BEYOND
THE ABYSS

A Spine-Tingling Collection of
SCIENCE FICTION
Short Stories

All Stories Written by

LYNN MICLEA

BEYOND
THE ABYSS

A Spine-Tingling Collection of
SCIENCE FICTION
Short Stories
Written by Lynn Miclea

***

Other Short Story Collections by Lynn Miclea:

ISBN: 979-8359319164
Independently Published

Cover photo from Pixabay.com

DEDICATION

This book is humbly dedicated to friends, family, and all my readers and supporters throughout the years who have believed in me, supported me, loved my stories, and given me encouragement when I needed it most.

And to my husband, Dumitru, for his patience, love, and undying support as I spent all my free time working on my books, struggling to find my way and make it all work.

Thank you all. Your support is very appreciated.

FOREWORD

Science Fiction is a popular genre that opens up incredible worlds to explore. It expands the imagination into fascinating alien planets, strange and frightening beings, captivating alien worlds, travel through time and space, and compelling adventures that boggle the mind.

I sincerely hope this collection of science fiction short stories does all that for you and much more.

Sit back and get ready to dive into these exciting, spine-tingling, and thrilling stories.

Thank you for stepping into *Beyond the Abyss*.

— Lynn Miclea
Author

TABLE OF CONTENTS

PORTAL

Ted entered the long portal station. Using the portal always gave him the heebie-jeebies. Although it looked like a strange train station, he knew what it was for. And he knew that too many things could go wrong. Especially where he was going.

Xardulan—a planet accessible only through a wormhole using this portal. It was all carefully monitored by the government, and he knew it should be safe. But it always unnerved him. And who knew what he would find when he got where he was headed? He knew he was only being sent there because something had gone wrong.

Working for the government was not easy. He was often kept in the dark, and everything was on a need-to-know basis. Yesterday, his boss had called him into his office and explained the experiments the government had been engaged in. Ted felt his skin crawl as he listened to the agreement they had reached with alien beings on Xardulan.

They had been supplying the aliens with human DNA to help create a new cross-species—a hybrid—that was supposed to have the best traits, abilities, and characteristics of both species. But something went wrong. The aliens had stopped communicating. They no longer responded to requests for information, and Ted was now being sent to check it out and see what was happening.

Nervous and agitated, he checked his watch. He was a few minutes early. The shuttle that ran in the portal would be there any minute. He wished a colleague could have come with him, but his boss insisted he go alone. That sent a shiver of fear through him. Backup was crucial. No one should ever go alone. Was it that dangerous that they didn't want to risk two people?

A high-pitched whirring sound announced the arrival of the shuttle—it was right on time. Ted noticed it was the larger shuttle this time, and he wondered why. He licked his dry lips and prepared to board.

The large shuttle eased to a gentle stop and the doors opened with a whoosh. Glancing around, he confirmed that he was the only one in the station. After hesitating for a moment, he stepped on board and heard the doors close. The shuttle was empty. He checked his watch and went to the controls, entering the proper coordinates and codes. Then he sat in one of the seats.

His stomach churning, he swallowed past the lump in his throat. He hoped this went well. But something told him there was a problem. A problem even greater than what his boss had implied. Again, he wished he had a partner coming with him. Going alone was always dangerous and ill advised, even without any possible issues.

Worries about what he might find filled Ted's thoughts as the shuttle took off and picked up speed. Would the aliens or the hybrids be violent? What were they being used for? Were the hybrids now trained war machines? What went wrong? Or maybe they didn't even survive and they were all dead. He shuddered. Whatever it was, he would deal with it. And he hoped it would be coming back soon.

After a thirty-minute ride through the wormhole, the shuttle eased into a station at the other end and came to a stop. With a soft whoosh, the doors slid open.

Ted paused and then stepped off the shuttle onto a platform. It was quiet in the portal station on this world. No one seemed to detect him or be aware that he had arrived. Strange and indistinct sounds from the surface reached him. He couldn't put it off any longer. Gritting his teeth, he walked forward and saw a moving platform leading to the surface.

Feeling jittery and anxious, he stepped onto the platform and it slowly brought him up to ground level. What would he find? Would he be safe?

Once the platform arrived at ground level, he got off and quickly moved to the shade of a nearby building and took in the scene. Relief moved through him as it seemed no one noticed him or knew he was there, and he simply observed for a few minutes.

What appeared to be human beings, wearing white gowns, were working hard doing manual labor. They looked entirely human. Was that possible? They were digging, planting, moving things, and building structures—groups of them working on specific tasks. What were they doing? Were they hybrids and it was just hard to tell from where he was? They sure looked human. Purely human.

A large blue creature with four elongated arms came into view. Tall and strong, towering over the humans, it barked orders in a strange language, yelling at the human workers. The humans cowed in fear and then worked faster, looking scared and unhappy. What was going on here?

He gasped as it suddenly hit him. They were not hybrids— they were human slaves. The aliens did not use the DNA to create a new species—they used it to have an ongoing supply of workers to do manual labor for them.

The pit of his stomach fell, and he stared in horror. He had to save them and get them out of there. No question about it. If they were human, he needed to help them.

The large blue creature finally left, and the humans seemed to relax and work a bit easier. But how could he communicate with them? He didn't know their language, and they would not know English.

Telepathy—he could communicate telepathically. Hopefully these humans were evolved enough to be able to communicate that way as well.

Ted focused on the closest human, a male who seemed to be in his early twenties. He focused his thoughts. *Hello?*

The human's head jerked up. He turned and looked around and then spotted him. His eyes widened, and Ted could feel the man's fear and confusion.

Ted quickly sent calming thoughts. *It's okay, I won't hurt you.*

The man stared for a few moments and then returned to his work.

Ted tried again. *Can I talk to you?*

The man glanced around and then slowly came over to Ted. The man's thoughts echoed in Ted's head. *Who are you? I have not seen you here before.*

Ted held up his hands in a peaceful gesture and smiled. "My name is Ted. What is your name?" He hoped spoken speech would be translated telepathically.

"I am S-3562. Where are you from?"

Ted spoke slowly. "I come from another world. A place where you originated. I am the same species as you."

S-3562 studied him. "Why are you here?"

"How many of you are here? Are you treated well? Are you happy?"

The man stared for a few moments and then shook his head. "There are two hundred of us. What is happy? We work for the rulers. They yell at us. They hit us. They demand that we work until we are exhausted and cannot move. We have a little free time in the evenings. That is our life. That is all we know." He squinted. "Is that what it is also like where you are from?"

Ted ached for these people. "No. We are free. No one rules us or demands that we work. We choose what we want to do."

S-3562 looked confused. "How is that possible? How do you get food?"

Ted pursed his lips. "Are there women here too?"

"Yes. Females. They are assigned different tasks than we are." His voice grew softer. "I have heard them crying, but I cannot help them."

"When do you stop working? Can we meet later and talk?"

The man nodded. "Yes. We stop working when it is dark. Then we eat. Then we are free for two hours. Then we sleep. Then we start again the next day. The same schedule every day."

A flash of anger raged through Ted. He would not abandon these people. He shook his head. He had to help them. "Are there any more people like you here?"

"They create new people each month in a factory. We are created to serve the rulers. When we are no longer useful, we are discarded and a new person takes our place."

"Where is this factory where people are created?"

The man pointed in one direction. "A building over there. Not far. People are created and the rulers do scientific experiments on them."

Ted's jaw clenched. "Do you know what you are?"

"We are hu-man. We are here to serve the rulers. We have designated work assignments. My name stipulates my designation and assigned task."

"Do you get to rest, play, laugh, love, be free, or enjoy yourselves?"

S-3562 looked confused. "I do not understand. Those attributes are for the rulers, not for hu-mans. We are here to serve."

Ted's voice grew passionate. "No. You are more than that. Much more."

"I do not understand."

Frustration rose in Ted's gut. "Where and when can we meet in safety?"

S-3562 pointed to a building a short distance away. "There. In three hours."

"Can you have everyone there? The females too?"

"Yes. We will all be there."

Ted nodded and he let out a long breath. "Good. I will speak to all of you." He bit his lip. "Will it be private? No rulers?"

The man nodded. "Yes. Private. Just hu-mans." He glanced around. "I must return to my duties or I will be disciplined and possibly injured or terminated."

***

Ted remained in the shadows, watching and observing. From what he could see and feel from them, they were definitely human and were created to serve as manual labor for the large blue creatures who ruled the planet. Those creatures had clearly lied and deceived Earth. They did not create hybrids—they created slaves, an unlimited and unending supply. And he would make sure it ended today.

For three hours, Ted stayed hidden while watching the workers. He thought about what he would say to these people and how he could save them. Would they be willing to leave this planet? What if the blue creatures discovered him? And what would he report back to his superiors on Earth? What would he tell them? Maybe they already knew. Maybe that's why they had given him the large shuttle. And maybe that was why he had been sent alone. His boss did not want to risk more than one person falling into their hands if anything went wrong.

Only one thing was still unresolved, but he wasn't yet sure how to handle it. He needed to demolish the building where they created and experimented on the humans, and he needed to eradicate all the available human DNA these creatures had. All of that needed to be wiped out and totally destroyed. But how? He had no weapons or explosives on him. He needed to think about how to do that without putting anyone at further risk or jeopardizing his plan to safely get everyone out.

Finally, after three long hours, Ted stood before the two hundred humans stuck on that planet as laborers through no fault of their own. "Hi. My name is Ted. I am from Earth. I am human, just like you. You were created from DNA from people from my home planet."

He glanced at everyone, and they stared back at him, some looking confused, some worried, and some expressionless. "You are humans, and humans are meant to be so much more than workers. You are meant to feel, play, love, be happy, laugh, rest, be creative, sing, dance, and have fun." He glanced at the puzzled faces before him and then continued. "Humans are not supposed to be slaves to any other being. You are not meant to serve under another." He paused and then slowly emphasized his next words. "I can help you."

Ted spoke to them for an hour, going into detail about how he wanted to help and what he was offering them. Then he answered questions, and the people started growing more animated. They seemed to come to life and get excited. Many were unhappy but didn't know how to change anything, expressing that this was all they knew, and they had no say in it and no choice. They were not allowed to disobey or step out of line. A few said they dreamed of escape, but it seemed impossible. Emotions came to the surface—confusion, anger, rage, and frustration. By the end of the hour, they were all on board with his plan. They were ready.

Frustration churned in his belly. He had not yet figured out how to destroy that one building. He hated leaving any loose ends, especially leaving human DNA behind. That was unacceptable.

"Thirty minutes," Ted reminded them as he wrapped up the meeting. "Meet me at the agreed-upon spot in thirty minutes. Bring whatever personal items you want to keep. You will not be returning. Everyone understand?"

Heads nodded, and then everyone scrambled out of the building except for one man who approached him.

Ted faced him. "Do you have a question?"

The man nervously glanced around and then looked at Ted. "I will take care of the factory with the hu-man DNA."

"You can do that?"

"Yes. It is risky, but I will try." The man glanced around again and then rushed out of the building.

***

Thirty minutes later, Ted led the two hundred humans down the moving platform to the subterranean portal station. The shuttle was waiting. It was large, but he now worried that everyone might not fit. And would the extra weight be a problem? He had never transported that many people before. Were his superiors expecting this?

The humans gasped and pointed. Their excitement was palpable.

"Okay, everyone, if you want to come with me back to Earth, please board the shuttle quickly, and we will be on our way. If you would prefer to stay here, you may do so. I am not forcing you. You are free to decide what you want."

Murmuring among themselves, they all quickly boarded the shuttle, squeezing in to fit. Ted glanced around the station. Not one person remained behind. He smiled to himself and then jumped as a loud explosion on the surface reached him, rumbling through the ground, with dust raining through the opening. *What was that?*

Shrieks erupted on the surface. Another explosion, followed by unintelligible speech.

Ted quickly jumped into the shuttle, closed the doors, and worked the controls, setting the destination and entering the codes. Three blue creatures came into view, racing down the moving platform as the shuttle whirred and the lights flickered. The creatures held strange weapons as they rushed toward the shuttle.

Come on, come on, Ted thought. *Let's go, let's go.*

A loud shriek sounded outside the shuttle and something banged on the shuttle door. Would the creatures damage it? Could they get away in time without a problem?

A vibration moved through the shuttle. The large vehicle started moving and rapidly picked up speed. Colorful streaks filled the viewscreen. They were on their way.

Ted let out a huge sigh of relief and looked back at the human refugees on board. Some looked worried, but most were smiling. A sense of nervous joy and anticipation permeated the air.

He looked at the nearest person, the man who had approached him at the end of their meeting. "What was that explosion on the surface? Do you know what that was?"

The man smiled, his face lighting up with glee. "We did it. We destroyed the factory where they created us. They will not be able to create any more hu-mans or experiment on us. And all the hu-man DNA was destroyed as well."

Ted clapped his hands and laughed. "Really? You did that?"

"Yes." The man nodded. "Three of us have wanted to do that for a while, so we were prepared. We knew what to do, and this was our chance." He smiled, a look of pride on his face. "Now we are finally free."

"Yes, you are." Ted turned back to the controls and sent a quick message to his immediate superior, explaining that he was bringing back refugees.

Twenty minutes later, the shuttle eased into the station and came to a halt. Ted turned to the control panel and re-set the coordinates and codes so that no unauthorized beings could follow him there and access the portal in the Earth station.

Then he turned to the group and raised his hands for attention. "Welcome home, my fellow humans. You are now truly free. I will bring you to my superiors and you will be welcomed and honored."

The doors to the shuttle whooshed open and Ted led the humans into the terminal to take their first steps on their true home world.

As Ted led the humans away from the shuttle and toward the government building entrance, his superior sent a return message to Ted at the shuttle, but Ted was no longer there to receive it.

DO NOT—repeat—DO NOT bring the refugees from Xardulan to our building. They must first be decontaminated against any possible alien disease. Also, a WARNING—we have reason to believe that one of them has brought a weapon with him that could decimate all life on this planet. Repeat—STAY WHERE YOU ARE. Please confirm.

Thirty yards from the shuttle, Ted smiled at the refugees as he led them into the government building below ground level. "Follow me, please," he said, approaching a bank of elevators. Satisfaction filled him as he glanced at the refugees. He knew his superiors would be happy, and he felt proud that he had brought them all home safely.

As he punched in his code and called the elevators to the subterranean level, he did not see one of the refugees at the back of the group reach into his bag and pull out a small device.

With a series of soft thumps, the elevators reached the ground level, and the doors slid open. Ted programmed all the elevators to access the fifteenth floor without any stops, and he then ushered all the refugees into the elevators, making sure they all entered and were accounted for. Then he entered one of the elevators with the last group of refugees. The doors slid shut with a gentle swish, and they began their ascent.

Brimming with confidence and excitement, Ted sent a message to his superior that they were in the elevators and on the way. He glanced at the refugees in his elevator car. He couldn't wait to meet with the management team and have these people properly received and taken care of. Everything was going better than he could have hoped for.

As the car rose to the fifteenth floor, one of the refugees in his car raised a small device and held it high above his head.

Ted's eyes opened wide as he stared at it. Alarm bells went off in his gut. *What was this guy doing? Did he pose a threat? Were they in danger?*

The refugee next to the guy with the device suddenly reached for the device, and the two refugees scuffled.

As Ted stared, terrified, trying to decide how to handle this, a white mist suddenly filled the car. Ted's eyes burned and his throat closed. He could not breathe. *What was happening? Was that from the device? Was it poisonous? Was he being killed? What had he brought back to Earth? What had he done?*

Panicked, Ted tried to hit the alarm button on the elevator, but he could not reach it. Weak, disoriented, his vision going dark, and unable to even gasp for breath, he collapsed to the floor.

***

One hour later, Ted woke up on a gurney, a doctor hovering over him. "Good," the doctor said. "You're awake. How are you feeling?"

Ted stared at the doctor and tried to speak, but only gurgling sounds came out.

The doctor leaned forward and removed the oxygen mask from Ted's face. "If you can't speak yet, that's okay. You will soon, don't worry." He checked his clipboard. "Are you in pain?"

Ted shook his head. Feeling groggy and confused, he looked around, noting the IV that ran into his arm.

The doctor nodded. "Yes, we have you on IV fluids and antibiotics. Don't worry, you're fine and all is well." He smiled. "All the refugees are being decontaminated, examined, and placed in quarantine, but we don't expect any problems."

"Wait," Ted said, struggling to get his voice working. "What was that mist that knocked me out? What happened?"

"Ah, that. It was our own protective device, a sedative that our security team administered to all the elevator cars, to put everyone in a light sleep and neutralize any threat. All of you will recover and be fine."

"It was not from any of the refugees?"

"No, that was from us, not them. Now you get some rest." He checked Ted's vital signs on the machine readouts and wrote in the chart he held on the clipboard. Then he looked up. "Ah, your boss is here to talk to you. Don't talk too long—you need your rest. I'll be back to check on you later."

As the doctor left, his white coat flapping behind him, Ted's superior entered the room.

"Ted," Captain Marcus Jamieson said, his stern demeanor showing rare signs of compassion.

"Hi, Captain."

"How are you feeling?"

"Okay, I guess. So that chemical that knocked me out was our own, not from one of the refugees?"

The captain nodded, his voice becoming professional again. "Yes. We had to take immediate precautions. That was very dangerous bringing them in like that."

Ted closed his eyes for a few moments and nodded. "I'm sorry, sir. Tell me, what was that device that one guy had?"

His supervisor cleared his throat. "We lucked out with that. It was a very primitive weapon, although it still could have hurt someone. We have it in custody." He crossed his arms. "He was scared of us and didn't trust what was happening, and he just wanted to protect himself. But that was a serious risk bringing them in like that, and it could have been much worse with dire consequences. That put us all in imminent danger." He paused, letting his words sink in. "But we were lucky this time."

"I understand. I'm sorry, sir." Ted shifted his position, trying to get more comfortable. "And all the refugees are okay?"

"Yes, they are safe and will be quarantined for a week, and they will be extensively questioned and interviewed. But they are fine and will be treated well." He gestured to the machines beeping, showing Ted's vital signs. "It looks like you are doing okay too, and you will live." He chuckled, glanced around the room, and then lowered his voice. "Tomorrow morning you will be debriefed. And in one week, when the refugees are out of quarantine, there will be a big welcoming ceremony for all the new arrivals."

"I'm glad they are okay. And I know I messed up there. I'm sorry."

The captain's voice softened. "Don't worry, everything is fine and everyone is safe. You did a good job with rescuing them and bringing them back. I'm proud of you, Ted. Job well done."

Ted gave a thumbs-up sign and tried to smile. "Thanks, Captain."

"Thank you, Ted. And welcome home."

~~~

DROP-OFF POINT

Katy stumbled as the burly man, his strong grip on her unrelenting, roughly pulled her across the hot sand. Quickly catching herself and regaining her balance, she stumbled after him over the yielding and uneven ground. Dust blew in gusts across the sand as they trudged forward.

She shook her head, vaguely remembering being grabbed, drugged, and thrown into the back of a car. She had awoken groggy and with a headache as the car came to a stop. This man had yanked her out of the car and was now marching her across the hot desert.

"Where are we? Who are you?" Her voice came out weak.

The man glanced at her, a stern look on his weathered face. "We're where we need to be. And it doesn't matter who I am."

She tried again. "At least tell me your name. And why we are here."

His grip tightened on her arm as he pulled her along. "My name's Grant, but that's not important. You're about to go on a little adventure." His raspy voice sounded menacing.

Her eyes burned and her muscles felt fatigued and weak. The drug had not completely worn off yet. "But I don't understand. What do you want?"

"This is the drop-off point. We wait here. See that?" He pointed into the distance. "They'll be here to get you."

"Who? For what?"

His lips curled into a sneer. "It doesn't matter."

Defiance and anger rushed through her. "Of course it matters! I have a right to know what is happening to me!"

Grant glared at her. "You are an offering."

She stared at him, not comprehending. "What?"

"An offering to alien beings. I bring them specimens, and they take you."

Katy peered into the distance trying to see. "Alien beings? Specimens?"

A large metallic object now shimmered into focus, and three strange green-gray creatures stood in front of it. Katy stared at it as panic coursed through her.

"Yes. They require human specimens."

Her voice shook. "For what?"

"I don't know and I don't ask. That is not my problem. I bring humans, and they give me—"

"No!" She struggled and tried to pull away from his grasp but his grip was too strong. "I won't do this!"

Grant smirked. "Where will you go? We are miles from nowhere. You cannot escape."

Katy glanced back at the alien spaceship, now clearly visible, and the hairs on her neck stood out. She felt her bowels loosen, and her breath caught in her throat. "Is that ..."

"That is their spaceship. They are coming here to collect you. Just like the others."

Her eyes widened in horror. "No!" She struggled again, desperately trying to get out of his grip.

The sound of a gun cocking cut through the struggle. She gasped and turned, her fear intensifying. Two men stood behind them, weapons trained on them.

One of the men gestured with his gun. "We will take her from here."

"No!" Grant shouted. "That is not the deal. I deliver her to them. Only me."

Seeing Grant distracted, Katy quickly twisted and bolted out of his grip, running a short distance away. But who should she trust? What was happening? Who were these two men with guns? Whose side were they on?

Needing to get away and have time to think, she sprinted, trying to get a good distance from them. A strong arm grabbed her. "Not so fast." She looked back to see one of the men with the guns.

Her throat constricted. "I just ..." Her body felt weak. Nausea rose into her throat. She wasn't sure if it was terror, lightheadedness from the drugs, or the heat of the sun, but she started feeling woozy. She stumbled, her body trembling and weak.

The man caught her and held her for a moment. "Are you okay?"

"Who are you?" she whispered.

He smiled. "My name is Kent, and my partner is Nick. We are investigators, undercover officers. We've been watching this guy for a while." He gestured toward Grant who was now being handcuffed by Nick. "We need to get you out of here."

Movement caught Katy's eye and she saw two alien creatures approaching, roughly one hundred feet away.

Kent stepped in front of her. "Stay behind me."

Katy peeked around the officer and saw the creatures raise weapons. She closed her eyes as the loud crack of gunfire filled the air. She jumped and whimpered, her body shaking.

Kent quickly turned to her. "Let's go—now. I need to get you back to our van. You'll be safe there." He grabbed her hand and pulled her toward a small mound of red sand.

Katy looked at the vast desert, confused. "Where is your van?"

"Here." He pulled her behind the mound of sand, and Katy looked back and realized there was a large reflective shield that camouflaged the vehicle behind it, appearing from the front like a broad, continuing expanse of the desert.

Katy glanced back at the creatures. The two alien beings and their spaceship shimmered and disappeared.

"What the—"

Kent opened the door to their van, and Katy noticed a trailer hitched behind it. "Get in. You'll be safe here. I'll explain more in a few minutes."

She slid in, feeling herself begin to calm down. She watched as Kent strode back across the desert and then returned a couple minutes later with his partner, who held tightly to Grant, his hands handcuffed behind him, as the officer pushed him forward toward the van.

Nick brought Grant to the trailer hitched in the back, and Katy watched as Grant was shoved into the trailer. Clanking sounds reached her as Grant was secured in the trailer. Then Kent and Nick took down the reflective shield, compacted it, and placed it in the back of the van. Kent got in the driver's side and Nick slid into the passenger's seat, glancing at Katy in the back seat and nodding at her.

Kent looked at his partner. "Is he secured?"

"Yes," Nick answered. "He's clamped into the restraints. He won't go anywhere."

Kent started the vehicle and then turned to Katy. "Are you okay?"

Katy nodded. "Yes. What is going on?"

Kent hesitated and then spoke slowly. "This has been taking place for a while. We are part of a sting operation to catch these men and the aliens, who the men are helping. The aliens have been landing in different places here in the desert, and it is hard to catch them, as they have advanced technology and shimmer in and out of existence. Even shooting them—they seem to heal and simply shimmer out, but then they return."

He paused and then continued. "We have now caught Grant, one of the men who have been bringing humans to them. But there are at least two more we are watching. We know how they operate, and we will catch them. We will come back here and end this for good."

Katy swallowed hard and licked her dry lips. "Why was I picked? And am I still in danger?"

He shook his head. "People seem to be picked at random. You are one of the lucky ones—we got to you in time. There are others who we could not get to fast enough to save, and they have not returned."

Katy shuddered as the van moved forward, bouncing over the sand.

A hissing sound suddenly filled the van and a green-gray alien shimmered into existence on the back seat next to Katy.

She gasped and whimpered, throwing herself against the door, as terror flooded through her. Nick quickly turned around, held up a large weapon, and shot the alien in the chest. The alien's eyes opened wide and then it shimmered out of existence and was gone, leaving a vague acidic odor behind.

Another whimper escaped Katy's lips. "What ... what ..."

Nick raised his eyebrows. "This ammunition that I'm using has a timed delay. Wait for it."

Katy's brow wrinkled. She couldn't figure out what he was saying. Looking out the side window, her eyes scanned the sandy desert. A few seconds later, the spaceship shimmered into existence, and then a powerful explosion rocked the desert. A deep boom traveled through the ground and the air, rattling the vehicle. Katy clamped her hands over her ears against the loud noise of the blast as shards of metal rained down on the hot sand. Her eyes wide, she stared where the spaceship used to be.

"Got it!" Nick stated, pointing at the debris in the desert. "Finally!"

Kent braked and looked at his partner. "Great shot—we did it!" He raised one hand and they high-fived each other.

Katy cleared her throat. "Was that the—"

"That was the spaceship," Kent explained. "We have now destroyed it. Hopefully we are finally done."

Nick motioned toward the trailer behind them. "Except for booking Grant. And the other two men. And the paperwork."

"Yeah, always the paperwork," Kent murmured, as he pressed on the gas and the van picked up speed.

Katy took a deep breath and felt sweat trail down her neck. She could easily have been on that spaceship. "Thank you," she said softly.

"You're welcome." Kent glanced in all directions around the desert. "Now let's hope there was only one spaceship and it's really over."

Katy gasped, her throat dry. "What?"

"We'll keep watch for a while. We hope this is it, but you never know—we don't know who we're dealing with or what they're capable of."

She nodded and bit her lip, gazing out the window at the golden desert sand flying by, as a shiver ran up her spine.

~~~

MANIFESTING

Alec sat down to write, excited about his new story. The thriller he was writing would be filled with action, and multiple battle-filled scenes ran through his mind as he thought about how he wanted his story to unfold. Although only sixteen years old, he was determined to be a great writer one day.

He added to his story, scribbling about a bad guy having a horrific car accident with the car catching fire and killing him. Satisfied, he put the pages away to finish later. It would be an exciting story, but he had other things he needed to do first, and he pushed away from his desk to take care of a few chores.

An hour later, he put the TV on to watch the news. After hearing politics and the weather, he was about to turn off the TV when a speeding car on the screen got his attention. As he watched, he saw the car crash and burst into flames. His eyes widened as he watched—it was so similar to what he had written earlier that day. A bizarre coincidence, but it held his attention and made his stomach flip. Paramedics arrived on scene, and Alec watched as they dragged the man out of the car and started doing chest compressions on him. Alec knew right away the man was not going to make it. It was exactly what he had written.

He swallowed hard. "Just coincidence," he muttered to himself. Then he returned to his room to continue writing, and he wrote into the evening.

***

Bright sunlight streamed through the windows the following morning as he got up. Alec finished breakfast and then ran back to his room to continue writing. He had a great new idea to add to his story, and he wrote about a powerful thunderstorm moving in. He glanced out the window—it was bright and sunny and a beautiful day, and he chuckled and continued writing.

An hour later, the light grew dim, and a low rumble sounded in the distance. He peered out the window. Huge, heavy gray clouds filled the sky. *What?* The weather forecast called for sun all day—no storms were forecast for that week. What was happening? He stood up and stared out the window. A brilliant flash of lightning lit up the sky, and a loud boom of thunder immediately followed.

Goosebumps rose on his arms, and he stared at his desk and the paper filled with the words of his story. It made no sense. It was bizarre, but it still had to be a coincidence.

Just for fun, he quickly scribbled on the paper that a dog barked and a car horn sounded. Shaking his head and snickering, he started getting up and then stopped short. The sound of a dog barking outside and then a car honking filtered through his window. *Impossible.*

He decided to test it further. He called down to his mother. "Mom? What's for dinner tonight?"

His mother's voice answered. "I'm making lasagna tonight. Why?"

"No reason, just asking."

He quickly sat down at his desk and wrote that the main character ate chicken for dinner. Then he continued with his story.

At dinner time, he went down to the kitchen. It did not smell like lasagna. His mother placed a large sizzling platter of baked chicken on the table.

Alec stared at it. "What happened to the lasagna?"

His mother laughed. "Oh, I don't know, I changed my mind and decided to make chicken tonight. We'll have the lasagna tomorrow night. Is that okay?"

His gaze shifted to his mom. "Yeah, sure, that's okay." The hairs on his neck stood up. *How could that have happened? Was he imagining it?*

His mother groaned and rubbed her hands. "Besides, my arthritis has been bothering me lately, and this just seemed easier." She put roasted vegetables and potatoes on the table and then sat down. "Well, eat up. I hope you like it."

Alec stared at the food. Was his writing causing things to manifest in the real world? Was he creating what was happening in real life? It couldn't be. That made no sense. It had to be just a very strange coincidence, even if it happened a few times.

He needed to test it again and decided to write something highly unlikely to happen. That evening, he wrote that he found a rowboat. That would never happen. Shaking his head, he continued writing his story.

The following morning was bright and sunny, and Alec decided to take a short walk through the woods which bordered a small lake a few blocks from his home. He loved hiking, and he always got creative inspiration when he walked in nature.

Cool, crisp breezes carried the scent of dirt, leaves, and shrubs, invigorating him as he entered the woods. It was an amazing day to walk, and he let his mind wander as he trekked through the wooded area.

As he rounded a curve on the dirt path, he gasped and stopped short. About twenty feet ahead of him, at the side of the lake, was an old abandoned rowboat. Quickly glancing around the area, he saw no one around. His heart in his throat, he slowly approached the boat. It was close to what he had visualized when he had written that he would find a rowboat. *What the—?*

Briefly inspecting the boat, he saw that it was dry and looked old, as though it had been abandoned long ago. He stepped closer and peered inside. It seemed to be in decent condition, but he was unsure what to do.

Shaking his head and glancing around, he threw his hands up and asked the air around him, "What does this mean? What is going on?"

Hearing no response, he looked back in the boat and bent forward, wondering if he should push it into the water and if it would be safe. As he watched, a piece of paper materialized on the seat.

Hands shaking, he stepped into the boat and lifted the paper. One word was printed on it: *"COME."*

"Come?" His mouth was dry and he felt shaky. "Come where? Out on the lake in the boat?"

Another paper appeared. *"YES."*

His stomach churning with fear and worry, and against his own logic and better judgment, Alec felt that he needed to see this through. He needed answers. He saw two oars in the boat and figured he could always paddle away if needed. After hesitating for a couple of minutes, he finally eased the boat into the water and climbed in.

Sitting on the seat, he picked up the oars and gently paddled out into the lake. As he started paddling to the left out toward the main area of the lake, the boat turned on its own to the right, around the shore, and headed for a small island a short distance away.

Alec desperately tried paddling in the other direction, but the boat continued on its path.

He called out, "Where are you taking me?"

A whispery voice sounded in his head. *"We need to correct a mistake."*

"I don't understand. What mistake? Who are you?"

There was no answer, and the boat continued to move toward the island. Alec's stomach knotted up as his anxiety increased. *Where was he being taken? Who were these people?*

About fifteen minutes later, the boat pulled up onto the shore of what appeared to be a deserted island covered with sand, scrub brush, and a few scattered trees. His stomach churning and his heart pounding, he sat in the boat for a few minutes without moving. Surveying what he could see of the island, it appeared quiet with no detectable movement.

Finally, he got out of the boat and pulled it farther up onto the shore so that it would be secure. Glancing around, he had no idea where to go. He took a few steps along the beach for a better look. There seemed to be a small footpath leading into the interior of the island where the trees were more dense, and he felt that was where he was supposed to go.

Slowly plodding along, he kept looking around for danger. Only the sounds of insects, birds, and rustling brush surrounded him. After walking for a few minutes, he saw a small hut hidden among a few trees. He stopped and stared. Was that where he was supposed to go? What was there?

"Come." The words echoed in his mind. *"We will not hurt you."*

His legs felt rubbery and weak, and he forced them to move and walk forward. As he got closer to the cabin, strange clicks and pops sounded from inside. A strangled gasp came from him, and he started backing up. *No, no, no, this could not be good.*

A strange, alien, insectoid-looking creature peeked out of a small window of the hut.

"Come."

Wanting to scream, turn, and run, his body froze and then seemed to move forward against his will, plodding up to the cabin door, which creaked open as he approached.

A large insect-like creature with huge, shiny black eyes stared at him and then stepped back, inviting him in.

Words filled Alec's mind. *"We have been observing humans. However, during this process, we inadvertently transmitted a specific ability to you that you have discovered through writing. This is not acceptable and we need to take that power back."*

Alec stared at the strange creature. "So it's true? I've been creating reality by writing it?"

"Yes. What you write gives it power to manifest." There was a pause. *"That is dangerous and cannot be allowed to continue."*

"But why do I need to come here in person? Couldn't you just—"

40

"*Extraction is more meticulous and difficult, and it is safer in person.*"

Alec's mind raced. Before they took this power away, he grabbed his pen and small notebook from his pocket and quickly scribbled on the paper. *I have a lot of money in my bank account. My mom is healthy and free from pain. I have—*

His fingers went numb and his mind felt confused. He could no longer write. He couldn't think of what he was doing. An intense pressure filled his head and he squeezed his eyes shut, shoving the pen and paper back into his pocket. He held his breath.

The pressure eased and a voice filled his mind. "*We apologize for this. It is our fault and should not have happened. You will have no ill effects. We wish you well. You may now return home.*"

Alec opened his eyes. He was on the shore of the island, standing in front of the rowboat. *What just happened? How did he get there?* He couldn't quite remember, but he knew he needed to get back home.

He pushed the rowboat slightly into the cool water and then climbed into the boat. Picking up the oars, he paddled out into the calm water. Why was he out there on the lake? He was not sure, but it was a nice day, and he paddled forward, sensing the right direction.

The lake opened up, and familiar woods appeared on his left. He knew instantly that's where he belonged, and he headed for it. As the boat reached land and stopped in the shallow water, he got out, pulled the boat up onto the shore, and looked around. He was not sure what had just happened, but he knew something significant had taken place.

Realizing where he was on the wooded path, he easily found his way out and to the small parking area and sidewalk. Walking the few blocks home, he put his hands in his pocket and felt the small notebook. He remembered writing something important. He quickly pulled it out and looked at what he had scrawled on the paper.

I have a lot of money in my bank account. My mom is healthy and free from pain. I have—

He remembered writing that! Rushing home, he raced to his room and turned on the computer. Quickly checking his bank account, he saw a recent deposit and a huge balance in his account. *Was that for real?* He ran downstairs. "Mom?"

His mother came out of the kitchen, a spring in her step. "Yes, dear?"

"How are you feeling? You look like you're feeling better."

"Yes, for some reason, I feel much better. Nothing hurts." She flexed her fingers. "Let's hope this lasts. It feels good to be pain free for a change." She smiled. "Ready for lasagna tonight? I'm making garlic bread, too."

"But—"

"Hey," his mother added. "How's your writing coming?"

Alec gave a weak smile. "It's great. It's a good story." He felt shaky. He knew he could never explain what had happened with the things he had written and have anyone believe him, and he decided not to mention it. "I'm glad you're feeling better."

He turned and ran back to his room. He needed to work on his story, but something kept tickling at the edges of his mind. Strange, vague memories of large insects, but he couldn't quite grasp it. He shivered and then shook it off.

Needing to test out the writing again to make sure, he quickly wrote that a dog barked. Silence answered him. Tilting his head, he carefully listened again, but he did not hear any dogs barking.

Breathing a sigh of relief, he knew one thing—just to be safe, he would make sure his story had a happy ending.

~~~

FINAL ASSAULT

Paul glanced at the tower above him, a smirk crossing his face. It was almost time to check in. He was sure his team knew—they monitored everything. He needed to send in a report and then return to his home base for a short while.

Taking out a hand-held device, he punched in a code, then a string of instructions. Satisfied that all was well, he put it back in his pocket. This was going better than planned. He looked up at the tower again, grateful for what it did for his people.

As he turned to leave, one thin man with a moustache approached him. "Hey, what are you doing?"

Paul sucked in a breath. "Nothing, sir, I am a maintenance technician. Just checking to be sure everything is functioning properly." He hoped that would satisfy this man.

The thin man stared at him, a strange look on his face. Paul felt a nervous quiver in his belly. Did this man suspect anything? Could there be a problem? He quickly nodded at the man, said a quick, "Good day," and turned to go home. He hoped the man accepted what he said without any suspicion. He was not sure. He was too close to the end to let anyone interfere or stop him.

Walking quickly to his small house, he scanned the area to make sure he wasn't being followed. Not seeing anyone, he entered the house and shut the door, and then let out a long breath. It was good to have privacy again and feel safe, even if it was in a temporary strange dwelling. An Earth home.

None of the furniture on this strange planet quite fit his body comfortably, even with a temporary human body, but that was to be expected. The furniture was really for show, in case someone visited or looked in the windows. Everything would look normal to these humans.

He went into the kitchen and looked in the fridge. A jar filled with slimy, crawling worms and bugs was in there, tantalizing him, making him realize how hungry he was. He grabbed the jar, unscrewed the lid, and shook a few morsels of delectable, squirming bugs into his mouth. Relishing the feel and the taste, he slowly chewed and swallowed, and then he placed the jar back in the fridge.

Paul entered the closet in the second bedroom, which had been renovated to suit his needs. It now contained a system of computers, which functioned as a center of operations, and a portal. Several specialized computers and communication devices, more powerful than anything that was developed on this backward, juvenile, and unsophisticated world, lined one wall.

He sat on the wooden chair, filled out a report of his findings, and sent it to his supervisor. His boss would be pleased. He had done a good job on this strange planet, investigating and infiltrating the lowly human defenses.

Turning toward the control panel along the back wall, he punched in his code, hit a few buttons, entered the target code, and held the handle on the transport device. Everything around him fluttered and turned misty white, and then slowly dissipated.

Letting out his breath, he exited the small receiving chamber on his home world and strode down the long familiar metallic hallway. He breathed in deeply the sharp, pungent air. It was good to be home. The Earth clothes hung in tatters on his long, scaly limbs as he returned to his normal appearance. No matter, he could always get more clothes when he went back.

A wide grin crossed his bony face as he entered a large office of glass and dark metal.

His boss was waiting for him, and the large, scaly reptilian creature leaned forward across his dark gray desk. "Partanelloq, welcome home. I've looked over your reports." He waved at Paul to take a seat. "Please tell me how your research on Earth is progressing."

Paul smiled. "It's going quite well. They call me Paul there, and they think I'm a maintenance technician. So far, no one suspects anything. I have observed and analyzed the habits of those archaic Earth humans. Very strange, infantile beings. They are at the beginning of their development and still have a long way to go. They have no idea who I am or what I am doing. And they have no idea what is coming."

The boss nodded, pleased with this report. "That is good. They really suspect nothing? Amazing. So we can move forward as planned?"

"Yes." Paul leaned forward eagerly. "I have infiltrated their computers, their communication devices, their weapons, and their so-called security measures, even at the highest levels. Even their weather has now been accessed and programmed. Everything is in place and ready. We can begin on your command."

Exhilarated, Paul sat back in his chair. Maybe he would even be promoted after this and be able to oversee the takeover of other underdeveloped planets himself, rather than do the legwork for others. But that could wait. He hissed in anticipation as he waited for his boss to respond.

The boss smiled, his sharp, pointed teeth glistening. "Excellent. I will give you one week Earth time to test out the areas we have infiltrated and see how it affects these Earthlings. Test out a different section and modality each day and report back to me. We will have them under our control very fast. They are no match for our intelligence or our technology."

"I agree, sir." A rush of pride and excitement filled Paul as he nodded. "It will be my pleasure to test out each area. These lowly humans won't even know what hit them."

The boss nodded. "Good, good. I look forward to your continued daily reports, Partanelloq. And then in one week, if all goes well, they can be annihilated and the planet will be ours."

Paul's tongue slashed back and forth as a hiss of excitement came out. "And I have your permission and authority to push the button for the final assault?"

The boss nodded. "Yes. It will be at your discretion." He hissed as his eyes lit up. "Thank you. You may go now." He waved a thin, scaly arm, dismissing him.

Paul got up, bowed in respect, turned, and left the office. Before he returned to that backward planet, he needed one good meal first. He made his way to the cafeteria, chatted with a few friends, and loaded up his plate with squiggly, squirmy creatures still covered in mud. Ah, a nice feast before he returned to Earth.

An hour later, he went down the long hall to the chamber, coded in the target of his small home on Earth, and pressed *Enter*. The air sparkled with a white mist, he felt the familiar vibration, and then the mist cleared. He found himself in the closet of his strange Earth home.

He had work to do. First, he checked on the tower that monitored various activity—electrical, mechanical, energetic, and human. All was working as planned. He hissed in delight. This was almost too easy.

Turning to his sophisticated computers, he programmed several sectors, hissed, and pressed *Enter.* Each section, one per hour, would affect communications, computers, and electronic devices. Then he would program and disrupt minor brain functions of the inept humans. Severe weather changes would come after that. The excitement was almost too much for him, and he could barely sit still.

Exiting the closet in the second bedroom, he walked to the front of the house and looked out the window, overlooking the street. He watched streetlights flash and go dark, as they malfunctioned. Unable to contain his glee, his hiss turned into a barking laugh. Incredibly excited, he kept constant vigil at the window. Car headlights went dark, and the sound of vehicular crashes reached him. *Excellent!*

The following day, Paul was thrilled as televisions, cable, and telephones in the city went dead. He watched as a neighbor stumbled out the front door of his house, confused, walking erratically. It was progressing splendidly. It was almost too easy.

He returned to the closet and his computer, checked the feedback from each sector, and made a few adjustments. Each day more sections of Earth would be infiltrated, controlled, and shut down. The excitement in him kept building. He checked the tower—it was working perfectly, monitoring and recording all electronics, all computers, all life, and all behavior of the backward humans.

He sent another report to his boss with all his latest findings and calculations. Murders had increased—people enraged and killing each other over nonsense. How could it be this easy?

That afternoon, a warning beep got his attention. Paul checked the information from the tower. The weather across Earth was changing sooner than expected. Fires, hurricanes, floods, tornadoes, earthquakes, and volcanoes all were becoming more active. He checked the controls again. That should not be happening yet—that was due days later, not now.

He reviewed the findings again and thought through the effects and ramifications. The fires and hurricanes had been scheduled to take place just before the end, not this soon. He adjusted the coding instructions. But maybe it wouldn't matter. It was only a few days away now anyway.

One day later, Paul allowed his body to start reverting back to its natural state. He clapped his bony hands together. The planet would be theirs within hours. The final assault was at hand. And he was in charge. He squawked gleefully, his tongue slashing back and forth. The mounting excitement was reaching a crescendo.

A loud crashing sound suddenly reverberated throughout the small house. *What was that?*

Voices reached him—human voices. "Where is he? The signals are coming from this house. We traced it back here."

Another commanding voice called out. "Search this place. Now!"

No! Nothing would stop him. It was too late for these humans to prevent what was about to happen on this backward planet, and the time was now. They could no longer stop this from happening. Paul's scaly fingers hovered over the key.

The humans made noise as they searched the small house, room by room. They were getting closer to the back room where he was. But they were too late, and it wouldn't matter anymore.

With a hiss of pure delight, he pushed *Enter* and gleefully waited for the shock waves to hit.

~~~

RESCUE

Alicia stared at the special communications receiver. Why wasn't he calling? Her husband had been at the lunar outpost for four months, and he had always called every day or two, even if it was just for a couple minutes at a time. But now it had been a full week without Drew calling at all, and it worried her.

Was he okay? Was he injured? Sick? Did he need help? Or was it a simple malfunction of the Earth-Moon-Earth device? The EME communication device had worked well until now. Moon bounce, the radio communications technique based on radio waves, had been reliable, and the slight echo delay didn't bother her at all. What had gone wrong? There were two other men with him there at the space station on the moon, but none of them called. Her stomach churned with anxiety.

The scientists at NASA were frantic at the lack of communication from the space station. They continually tried to reach the men. After forty-eight hours with no contact, they finally received a brief message by Morse code using the landing lights at the landing pad, but then nothing. They tried everything they knew, but could not reach them and they heard nothing else. Now desperate, three days later, they contacted Alicia and brought her up to date.

They let her know what was happening and, as she had been trained, they asked her to be on standby for going to the moon if needed. Everyone was deeply concerned, and it intensified her own fears. If NASA had lost communication with them, there could be a real problem.

She had been working closely with Drew on all the schematics and configurations for fixing and improving the in-situ resource utilization unit, or ISRU. She knew his work inside and out. And she had been trained and cleared as an astronaut as well. She desperately needed to go there. She was his partner in all aspects of his work, in addition to being his wife. If he was in trouble, she had to help him.

One day later, NASA called again and requested that she go to the moon, and she immediately agreed. She was the right person to go. If he needed help, whether with the work on the ISRU, the processor unit, rovers, robots, hydroponics, EME device, any of the other equipment, or even with something personal, she was the best person after Mitch and Steve, who were already there working with him.

After spending one full week in isolation to make sure she would not bring any diseases with her, the day was finally here. She felt nervous and fidgety. Anxiety flooded through her system. There was still no communication from Drew, and she desperately hoped he was okay. She hoped all three men were okay. She packed her research notes for what he was working on, food, change of clothes, and medical supplies. She sent an urgent prayer that her husband and his two colleagues were fine and not injured.

Gray clouds threatened rain on the morning of the launch, but they cleared by early afternoon, and the launch was on. Why was she so nervous? Something had to be wrong. She just felt it. She tried to ignore it, but the anxiety was insistent. She needed to be there as soon as possible.

"10 ... 9 ... 8 ... 7 ..." She gritted her teeth and closed her eyes. "... 4 ... 3 ... 2 ..." She gripped the armrest and squeezed. "... liftoff!" The rumble and shaking seemed to rattle every cell in her body, and the pressure was intense. Once it eased, all she could think about was her husband.

***

As soon as the shuttle was set down on the moon in the designated landing place, she double-checked and triple-checked all the components on her spacesuit and oxygen tank. Everything seemed to be okay.

Exiting the shuttle, her breathing reverberated in her ears, accompanied by the whoosh of her blood. It was incredibly exciting walking on the moon—a real thrill, and something she had always dreamed about. She wished she could enjoy and savor it instead of being in a hurry. Her steps were awkward and slow, and with the thin atmosphere and low gravity, each step bounced her up in the air. She almost fell several times. She tried to do hops like she had been taught, and that helped. She struggled to control her steps, doing the running hops, for the short distance to the modular station where Drew and the other two men worked. *Please be okay, please be okay,* she kept repeating to herself as she hopped forward.

After what seemed like a long time, but must have been just a few minutes, she entered the entry port to the building, closed the door to the airlock, and punched in the codes. She then shifted from foot to foot waiting for gravity, atmosphere, oxygen, temperature, and other necessary conditions to shift to Earth normal.

Finally! Alicia quickly peeled off her spacesuit and attachments, opened the door, and ran into the main lab of the module.

"Drew?" She looked around. Where was he? "Mitch? Steve? Drew?" Her voice grew louder and desperate.

There! Drew was slumped over one of the processors. Racing to get to him, she tripped on something but caught her balance. A pencil lay on the floor—that's what she had tripped on. She ignored it and rushed to his side.

She quickly glanced around the room. Mitch and Steve were lying on the floor. Dried foam was around their mouths, and their faces were blue. Dead. What had killed them? Whatever it was, Drew had it too. "Drew!" she shouted to his pale, sweaty face. At least he was still alive.

He moaned, licked his lips, and opened his eyes. His pupils widened as he saw his wife in front of him.

"Drew, what happened? What is wrong?"

He moaned again, tried to speak, and coughed. He pointed to the computer.

Alicia wiggled the mouse and the monitor lit up to show a document on the screen. Her eyes quickly scanned it, catching key words—*sick, weak, fever, coughing, headaches, EME communication out.*

"Drew, what happened to you?" She squeezed his hand and then felt his forehead. He was burning up. "I need to get you home. You need medical attention."

Drew's head nodded slowly. "Wa... water..." he whispered hoarsely.

"Yes, of course." Alicia ran to the small kitchen area, filled a glass with water, and brought it back, holding it to Drew's parched lips. "Here, drink a few sips."

He struggled to sit more upright and then sipped the water. Then he collapsed back onto the chair, his breathing rapid.

Alicia searched through her medical supplies. She knew she had brought antibiotics. Where were they? There they were! She took a few pills and brought them to her husband. "Drew, take these. They will help you."

She held the back of his head as he sat forward slightly. She pushed the pills into his mouth, and he sipped more water and swallowed. Then he sighed and leaned back.

"Drew, did you finish the work on the ISRU? Did you do what you came here to do? Is it all done? Did it work?"

A flicker of a smile touched Drew's lips. "Almost," he whispered. "Last phase. Almost done. Couldn't finish. Not much left ... lost focus ... couldn't concentrate ..."

Alicia moved to the computer. Drew's notes sat next to the keyboard. She skimmed the notes and saw exactly where he was. She searched the folders on the computer. There. He had entered all the calculations and made the modifications except for the last part. It was so familiar—they had worked on this exact part together. And she knew precisely what was missing.

Should she take the time to finish his work? She estimated a couple of hours to complete it, and she knew what he was working on was critical. But her husband was dying. Would she be putting his life at risk if she worked on it and delayed bringing him home? Then again, how could she come this far, know his work so well, and not finish it? She debated it for a few minutes and then got to work.

For the next hour, Alicia moved between the computer and the processors in the lab. She adjusted the parameters, checked the feedback, added the necessary computations and set the data input the way it should be. Almost done.

She ran back to Drew and gave him more water. He sipped it, coughed, and then rested.

Back to the processors. She entered the correct specifications for each module and each component. Made adjustments for the solar cells in the solar arrays. Another hour passed. Sweat dripped down her neck. Almost done. The last segment in the final sector ... *click.* Done!

A loud humming filled the room. It worked. It was now complete.

She knew the EME communications needed adjustments to the linear polarization in the antenna to get the moon bounce communication back up and running, probably due to interference, but she couldn't worry about that now. She had to get her husband home.

She returned to Drew. His skin was clammy. "Drew," she murmured. "Hang in there. I'll get you back home. Stay with me. Please."

Drew moaned and his head rolled back, his breathing shallow and rapid.

"Drew!" Alicia rubbed the back of his hand and patted his cheek. A low groan came from his lips.

She hefted him up, got him to the bathroom, and helped him relieve himself. She washed his face as he leaned against her and shivered.

"We have to get you home. Have you eaten anything?"

He did not answer. She searched the kitchen area and grabbed a few containers of water, juice, and soup.

"Let's go," she said, urging him forward. "We need to go home now."

She got him into the airlock at the entry port of the building, closed the door, and dressed him in his spacesuit. Then she put on her own. She checked all the settings multiple times and turned on his oxygen. She saw his breath fog up his mask. She made another adjustment and checked the settings again. Time to go. Did he still have time left? Would he make it back to Earth alive? A tremor of fear ran up her spine.

Alicia punched in the codes, waited, and then opened the door to the outside. Holding his arm, she pulled Drew after her. He stumbled forward, leaning on her. A small rover was just outside the door. She helped him get in, and then she scooted behind the wheel and drove it away from the module. It slowly tracked over the lunar surface toward the shuttle. Almost there. Finally reaching it, she turned off the rover, got out, and helped Drew out. He was so weak. Her hands trembled as she punched the buttons at the entry to the shuttle. She stamped on the ground with impatience. It finally opened. Yes!

Once in the shuttle's airlock, she set the controls and waited for everything to reach Earth specifications. Then she took off both their spacesuits, got back into the navigation section of the bridge, and buckled them into their seats. Drew moaned, and she gave him another dose of antibiotics and some water. "Hang in there, Drew. We'll be home soon. Please hang in there."

***

Drew lay in the ICU bed at the hospital near the Jet Propulsion Laboratory just outside Pasadena, California. Fluid dripped into him from the IV next to his bed. He lay listless and pale, an oxygen mask over his face.

A doctor entered the ICU and approached the bed, his white coat hanging open and a stethoscope around his neck. He nodded to Alicia. "You're his wife?"

"Yes. How is he?" She stood up, her body shaking.

"He has bilateral pneumonia, also known as double pneumonia. Both lungs are affected and are inflamed and filled with liquid. He also is in the first stage of sepsis, moving toward severe sepsis, which is dangerous and can be fatal. We are treating him aggressively with antibiotics, corticosteroids, fluids, and oxygen, and we are checking vital signs every hour. He is not yet in septic shock, but I will not lie to you—he is in critical condition. He can recover, but he can also go downhill. We will monitor him and do our best."

Alicia nodded and bit her lip. "But how could they have gotten sick there? They were in isolation before they went."

"I don't know." The doctor's voice was soft. "Possibly there was something they packed and took with them that had been contaminated and they didn't know. But whatever it was, we will do our best to help him."

She nodded. "Thank you, Doctor."

"And it was a good thing you brought him in when you did. He might not have lasted much longer without medical treatment."

***

Two weeks later, Drew was discharged and went home. Still weak, he reached for Alicia's hand as they sat across from each other at the kitchen table. "Thank you, Alicia. I can't believe I'm still here."

"Drew, I barely got to you in time. We were lucky. You didn't have much time left."

"And my two buddies—Mitch and Steve. I hated seeing them so sick. There was nothing I could do." He shook his head, tears in his eyes. "I watched them die," he added softly.

She searched his eyes, compassion welling up in her. "I'm so sorry. That must have been awful."

"What about their families? Do they know?"

Alicia blinked against the burning in her eyes. "Yes. NASA is notifying their families." She paused and then continued. "They will be sending out another shuttle with a crew to decontaminate the entire lab and bring both of them home."

Drew took a bite of his chicken sandwich. "I couldn't even call out for help. The EME communication system went down, and I didn't have time to get it fixed." He chewed and then swallowed. "Besides, the three of us were not feeling well by then, and we could barely focus. And the job we were working on was much more of a priority." He waved his arm at her. "How did you even know I needed help?"

"You stopped calling and I just knew. I knew something was wrong. I felt it." She sipped her iced tea. "And then NASA called me, and I couldn't get there fast enough."

"And my work on the ISRU—you finished it?"

"Yes. I could see exactly where you left off. I knew what needed to be done. It's all finished."

His eyes lit up. "And? Did it work?" He took another bite of his sandwich.

"Yes, it did!" She bit into her sandwich. "It worked perfectly, just the way we expected. You did almost all of the work, you got really close, and I simply finished it. But it worked exactly the way we thought it would. You are a genius." She smiled and took a big gulp of iced tea.

Drew chuckled. "I was almost a dead genius."

She laughed. "Almost, but not quite." She reached over and squeezed his hand. "Welcome back to life, Drew. You have a second chance. And I'm so proud of you."

He smiled. "I'm proud of you too, Alicia. You completed the work. That was so important. That lunar outpost needs to be a viable base of operations for a long time, and what we were doing was critical." He pursed his lips. "Not to mention you saved my life."

"I'm glad I got to you in time. It was close. Too close." She thought for a few moments. "We're a good team. And it sure is good to have you back here on Earth."

"You can say that again. This is the most beautiful planet in the universe, and it is so good to be back home."

"And still be alive."

Drew laughed. "Yes, being alive is a good thing."

Alicia leaned over and kissed him softly. "Welcome home, sweetheart."

~~~

TOWER OF POSSIBILITIES

D iane's breath came in fast, raspy gasps, and she stopped for a few minutes to rest and look around. The spiral staircase went up a long way, and her footsteps echoed in the tall, empty chamber. She shook her head and tears stung her eyes. Grief threatened to overwhelm her again.

She had just lost Robbie yesterday. He had been shot and killed in front of her, and it was her fault. How could she not have seen that coming? She should have prevented it. *Damn!*

They had been crouched behind the sofa during the agency's operation, hidden for the moment. The bad guy had entered the room from the left side. She knew the snipers would get the bad guy. *Finally.* This was the moment they had all prepared for. She held her breath.

And then Robbie started getting up. She grabbed for him, but he got up too quickly. The sniper fired. The bullet hit Robbie.

She gasped again at the memory, a deep aching wave of grief flooding her as she choked on a sob. *No!*

Diane resumed running up the stairs. It was a great place for both exercise and working off emotions, but it was not helping today. Would anything help? She doubted it. Not only had she been there to protect Robbie, but she had fallen in love with him, and he had recently moved in with her. He was the world to her. And now he ... he ...

She picked up the pace and continued up the stairs. As she ran, she noticed doors every now and then along the stairwell. Where did they lead? From what she knew, there were no rooms off this tower.

Glancing as she continued up, she noticed numbers on the doors: 1952 ... 1964 ... 1975 ... The numbers struck her as years, but that made no sense. What was happening?

Stopping at the next closest door, she looked at the number—1989. After hesitating for a few moments, she slowly opened the door. She found herself in a round chamber with twelve doors arranged around the circular wall. Each door had the name of a month on it. Confused, she stared at them as a shiver ran up her spine. She slowly backed out, entering the stairwell again. What was that room for?

Shaking her head, she continued up the stairs, and the doors kept appearing. 1996 ... 2004 ... 2012 ...

Finally reaching the top, panting and out of breath, she saw one last door. The current year. *Why?*

She opened it and entered the round chamber. Peering around the room, she saw twelve doors, each with the name of a month on it, just like the previous chamber.

Feeling drawn to the current month, she slowly opened the door, hearing it creak as it opened into another round chamber. This room contained numbered doors—the days of the month. She rushed to yesterday's door. Maybe she could change what had happened. Is that what the doors were for? Was she being given the chance to change what had occurred? Was that even possible?

Opening the door with yesterday's date, she saw it led to another round chamber containing rooms with the hours on their doors. Her heart pounding in her chest, she raced to the door with the hour before Robbie was shot.

Slowly opening the door, she peered inside. The room where it had all taken place opened before her. The sofa. Robbie. And there she was as well, crouched behind the sofa next to Robbie, her back toward her. Sweat broke out over her scalp.

Without thinking, she felt herself pulled into the room. She now felt whisper-light and floated toward her crouched body. She felt herself gliding through her back, drifting into her body.

She put her hand on Robbie's back, feeling the warmth of his body. She focused, alert and vigilant. Footsteps sounded in the room. The smell of an old cigar. She immediately knew the bad guy had entered from the side. It was going to happen. She knew the sniper was ready. It was about to go down.

Robbie shuffled and started to rise. *No!* She grabbed him and pulled him back. He fell against her with a thud.

The bad guy's voice rang out. "What—"

A shot pierced the air. A gasp and then something thumped to the floor. She peeked around the sofa—the bad guy lay on the floor, eyes open in shock, a red stain widening on his shirt in the middle of his chest. He had been hit by the sniper's bullet.

And Robbie was safe. Baffled, but safe. Relief flooded her system. *She did it!*

She felt herself drifting out from the back of her body. Looking back, she saw her body still holding Robbie. The bad guy was there sprawled on the floor ...

And then she was back in the stairwell. Did that actually happen? Had she saved him? Was this just a wild fantasy? Was she hallucinating?

Her mind ran through her recent memories ... This morning he had made scrambled eggs for her. But no, that couldn't have happened—she remembered making cold cereal by herself, and she was all alone ... what was going on? Nothing made sense.

Excited and hopeful, she turned and ran back down the stairs, trying not to go too fast. Nervous and jittery, she rushed and suddenly missed one step. Skidding, she fell hard on the next step. She stood, brushed herself off, and then continued down the stairs a bit slower, careful not to trip again.

New feelings flooded her. Fullness ... love ... mixed with a tinge of grief. She no longer knew what was real or what to believe.

Tears streamed down her cheeks. This was impossible. It could not have happened. She was delusional. It all had to have been a figment of her overactive imagination.

As she rounded a curve in the staircase, a wispy white cloud floated in the stairwell. Thoughts immediately filled her mind. *We have allowed you to make this one change, as it was needed to save thousands of lives in the near future.*

The cloud dissipated. What was that? Another idle fantasy? None of this was possible.

Her muscles straining, feeling sore and fatigued, she continued down the stairs and finally reached the bottom of the tower. Sweat beaded on her skin and she gasped for breath. Exiting the tower, she blinked in the bright sunlight. How could any of this have possibly happened? She must be simply having a wild fantasy. There was no way any of that could be true. It was all a wishful illusion, nothing more.

Shaking her head at her absurd fantasies, she rushed home. She had to get a better grip on what was real. She needed to face reality and what actually happened. She had lost Robbie yesterday. That was a fact. She refused to be lost in a delusion.

She slowed as she approached her house and hesitated at the front door. Her hand shaking, she opened the door slowly, as fear, desperation, and hope warred inside her.

Entering the house, she froze and then looked around. Her heart pounded and her throat constricted. It was quiet. He must not be ...

"Diane?" Robbie's voice called out.

"Robbie?" Her voice was barely a whisper.

"Hi, honey, how was your run?" He came out of the kitchen and his arms opened to embrace her.

Gasping and sobbing, she fell into his arms, feeling his warm body against hers. She buried her head in his neck, inhaling his familiar scent. *He was here!*

"I love you," she murmured into his chest.

Robbie laughed. "Hey, I love you too. And that must have been some run today."

"You have no idea," she whispered, tightly hugging him.

~~~

Lynn Miclea

HOPING TO HEAL

S cottie sighed. He hated being sick. What did he ever do to deserve this? Was he supposed to learn something from it? Every muscle in his body ached, and he was getting weaker. He could not see any point or find any silver lining in being sick, even though he tried. He would probably never feel well again, and he hated that.

He had been to two specialists, and they suspected a neuromuscular disease. They were still trying to figure out which one, and they did not yet give him a final diagnosis.

Not knowing what was wrong seemed to be even worse than knowing, but he also dreaded finding out and making the diagnosis final, a diagnosis for an illness that could possibly be fatal. A heavy despair settled in his belly.

Shaking his head, he slowly stood up, wobbled a bit, and grabbed the table for support. Then he straightened up and looked around the room for his wheelchair. Maybe he'd go out for a bit. It probably wouldn't be long before he couldn't walk at all, and going out would be much more difficult. He wanted to make the most of whatever time he had left while he could still move around fairly comfortably.

Deciding to go to his favorite place, he pushed his wheelchair out the front door, closed the door behind him, and then carefully sat in his wheelchair. After diligently pulling his feet onto the footpads, he started the journey, wheeling himself two short blocks to the beach.

Exhaustion already began to overtake him, and he rested there on the footpath along the beach, staring out at the sand, the ocean, and the long pier stretching out into the distance.

His eyes burned with tears of frustration. After a brief rest, he slowly rolled forward toward the pier, went up the short ramp, and started down the long walkway. This was his favorite place in the whole world, where all his troubles, worries, and fears melted away. He felt normal and whole here, and he treasured that.

In addition to loving this place, there was something in the water at the end of the pier that caught his interest and intrigued him to no end. A few months ago, he noticed a strange light in the water. A soft blue light that didn't belong there. Was it a fishing device? A motion detector or monitoring device? Or maybe something alien? Curious, he felt drawn to the pier more often to see what was happening.

Today was no different. And now that he was getting noticeably weaker every day, he didn't know how much longer he could make it out here. Fierce desire burned in him. Filled with determination, he pushed forward and wheeled himself down the long length of the pier. The brisk salty air washed over him and he listened to the waves crash onto the shore behind him. His arms ached with the effort, and he finally stopped ten feet from the end and took a deep breath.

Gazing out over the deep blue of the ocean, he felt like he was at the end of the world. There was nothing but peace and endless ocean. He felt part of all life here. He felt whole.

After resting for a few minutes, he struggled to get out of the chair, and he shuffled the last few feet to the end of the pier.

Taking a deep, calming breath, he removed his shoes and carefully sat at the edge, his legs dangling over the end of the pier. He felt free.

Were the lights here today? He peered into the depths of the water below him.

***

Drokan collected his data and meticulously entered the information into his onboard computer system. It was fascinating to study these humans, and he loved this assignment on Earth. They were a backwards species with violent tendencies, and he had been warned to keep a distance and never make contact with any of them. In fact, he was clearly warned to not let them even see him or know he was there.

That was fine with him. He was a scientist, and he made his observations and reported his data. Soon he would be off to his next assignment on another planet, and he wondered where that would be.

But while he was here, he focused on his work. However, there was one human who touched his heart. He was surprised by his reaction to this one, but for some reason, he felt for this human—the guy who came out onto the pier and sat at the edge.

Drokan worried that this guy might have noticed something odd in the water, but there didn't seem to be any danger, and he was convinced this human was not violent. Drokan was sure it would be okay, and he knew he would be leaving soon anyway.

It struck him that this human might be sick. It appeared that there was something wrong with his body, that it was not functioning the way it should. Drokan never mentioned this human to his superior. But this guy reminded Drokan of his own brother who had died a short while back. Drokan felt an affinity with this human who seemed to be lost and hurting. He wasn't sure why the human was sad and ill, but Drokan wanted to help him. No one should suffer like that, and if it was possible to help him, he would do what he could.

Drokan knew it would go against protocol and was not allowed, but the strong yearning to do something to help this one human kept building. He would need to be really careful to not be seen, that was all.

He would keep it out of his reports, and no one would know. He just needed to figure out how to get the proper medical treatment into this guy's body. His mind ran through a few options, and he carefully considered how to do it.

***

Scottie stared into the water. There seemed to be that familiar soft blue glow coming from the depths, but he wasn't sure. Maybe he was seeing things. Maybe all of it was his imagination. Or maybe he was hallucinating because of whatever illness he had that wracked his body.

He tried swinging his legs, but they were weak and barely moved.

For the hundredth time that day, he thought how much he hated being sick. If only there was a cure for whatever he had. Otherwise, maybe it was time to get his affairs in order. Pay his bills, close his bank accounts, cancel his credit cards, give away his possessions ... He shook his head, grief and longing flooding him.

Scottie closed his eyes and breathed in the fresh ocean air, letting it wash over him and take his fears and worries with it. He wanted to just sit there at peace and pretend all was well, even for just a little while longer.

After a few minutes, he peered into the water again. The blue light was brighter now. And there was a metallic object hovering in the water. He guessed it might be some type of vessel. It seemed to vibrate or shimmer. Goosebumps rose on his arms. *What was that?*

As he tried to focus more intently, the water abruptly rippled and a huge wave broke the surface, shooting into the air like a small geyser. As he gasped and his eyes widened at the sight, he leaned back slightly as the water curved over him and broke over the pier, soaking him with a rush of cold water. He closed his eyes and held his breath.

Something sharp suddenly pierced his left foot. *What the—*

He quickly sat up straight and his eyes flew open. As he looked into the water, a green scaly tentacle-like appendage hastily slithered down into the depths and disappeared. *What was that thing?*

Peering into the water, he saw the metallic vessel wobble and shimmer, and then it drifted deeper and was still again. He didn't like this, and worry gripped him.

He tried to look at his foot, but his leg did not have the strength to lift more than a couple of inches.

An icy finger of fear crept up his spine. *Was that poisonous to him? Was he going to die?*

As terror flooded his body, he scooted backwards, breathing hard, his heart thumping in his chest. Sitting there a few minutes, he glanced around but did not see anything unusual, and he tried to calm down. Was he okay? Nothing hurt, although the bottom of his left foot was a bit itchy. He felt okay. No pain, so maybe it wasn't poisonous.

He put his shoes back on and struggled to his feet, and he realized it was a little bit easier than usual to get up. Or maybe it was just fear that fueled him. He turned the wheelchair around to face back the way he had come, sat in the chair, put his feet on the footrests, and started back. He felt like he had a touch more energy than he had earlier, and it was a bit easier to move the chair down the pier. Or maybe it was just adrenaline from worry, he wasn't sure which. Either way, he moved a little easier down the walkway, down the small ramp, and to the footpath along the beach.

Twisting around, he peered back at the ocean. It looked calm and peaceful. He wasn't sure what had happened, but he felt a little stronger than he had earlier. With renewed energy, he wheeled himself the two blocks back to his home.

***

Drokan entered the latest data and sent the report to his superior. All final results for his job were now coded and tabulated, and he was finally finished with this assignment. There was one final report to send, and he would do that one shortly. All was well, and he was pleased. This was a job well done, and it was time to move on. Earth was fascinating and the humans were full of contradictions. But despite that, he had enjoyed this job, and he felt good. And on top of everything, he had helped heal that one human, and no one needed to know about it. It was now time for his next assignment, and he started preparations to depart the planet.

***

After getting inside his house, Scottie decided to make lunch. He had a burst of energy that he had not felt in a while, and it felt really good. He stood up from the wheelchair, steadied himself, and then walked into the kitchen. Not bad. Maybe this was just a good day. Or maybe it was the fresh ocean air that had helped. Either way, he felt a bit stronger and made a sandwich and a small salad.

As he sat down to eat lunch, he glanced down at his left foot, which was itchy again. The whole foot itched, not just the bottom of it, and that worried him. Pulling up his leg and then easing his sock down, he inspected his foot. As he stared at the top of his foot, his mouth went dry and he found it hard to breathe.

A small, raised mound appeared on the top of his foot. A green, scaly mound of crusty skin. It looked like ... like ... that appendage that had slithered down into the water ...

Horrified, Scottie gasped and stared at his foot.

Suddenly, he was no longer hungry.

Pushing his sandwich away, he stood and paced. He felt stronger and more energized, but at what cost? What was happening? He could not even bring himself to consider what that scaly bump might mean ... what it could imply ... what might possibly be happening ...

Trying to distract himself, he put on a movie, but could barely focus on it. When the movie ended, he realized he had not paid attention and could not even remember what it was about.

Getting ready for bed at night, he felt somewhat nauseous but was not sure if that was from fear, terror, the alien venom, or his illness. Overwhelmed with anxiety, he tossed and turned all night, hardly sleeping at all.

Bright sunlight streaming through his window woke him up the next morning. He got out of bed, feeling stronger and healthier than he had in a long time. No longer nauseous, he realized he actually felt good. Maybe he was finally healing from the illness. Whether it was from the alien venom or just his immune system, he didn't know, but he felt much better.

He stood up and stretched, feeling strong and stable. In the bathroom, he glanced at himself in the mirror. No longer pale, his cheeks shone with color. Maybe he really was getting better.

He shuddered as he realized his left foot was still itchy and there was a slight ache in that leg. An icicle of fear crept up his spine. He knew he needed to look. "Please ..." he whispered.

Garnering his courage, he glanced down at his left foot.

He gasped as shock ran through him. "NO!" he wailed, breaking out in a cold sweat.

The green scaly mass now covered most of the top of his foot and was half-way up his leg.

Panting heavily, he reached for the counter as his legs gave out, and he collapsed onto the floor.

A sob escaped him as his mind reeled with horror and panic. What could he do now? He couldn't go to a doctor. And he couldn't treat this himself.

There was only one thing he could do. He would return to the pier. Whether that creature could offer a cure or whether it would kill him and end this, he would be okay either way. He could not live with what was happening to him.

After getting dressed, he stretched and flexed his muscles. He felt strong and energized. Looking at his wheelchair, he wondered if he even needed it today. Maybe he could try walking to the pier this time, for the first time in a long time.

A bit nervous but energized, he left the wheelchair at home and walked the two blocks to the beach. As he reached the beach, he realized he was beginning to feel tired. He was not used to walking this far. Maybe this was a mistake. But it was too late now.

Scottie rested for a few minutes on a bench along the beach, and then slowly made his way up the short ramp and down the pier, letting the fresh ocean air wash over him. If the entity would help cure him of this alien infection, he would be strong and could easily walk back home. And if the creature made it worse, took over his body completely, or even killed him, that would be fine with him. He could not continue like this. He was ready to surrender to whatever would happen.

He sat down at the end of the pier, removed his shoes, and let his legs dangle over the edge. He took a deep breath and let it out slowly. Fatigue began to eat at him. He felt more than tired. Exhaustion overtook him. Maybe it was too soon to walk as far as he had. He was worn out. What was he even doing there? And how would he get back home? He felt agitated. This had to be a mistake. A huge mistake. Feeling overwhelmed, he wasn't even sure what he was doing at all anymore. Tears burned his eyes.

***

Drokan filed his final report. He was now done and he felt satisfied. He checked the ship's systems and controls one last time. He was ready to leave.

Wait. Something tugged at him. That human was back again. Something was wrong. What happened? His mind tuned in. He could sense it, and he considered possible options. He thought he might know what went wrong. Maybe he could help. He would make one last effort to help, and then he would leave.

***

Scottie stared into the water. That blue light was there again. He couldn't even remember what it meant. Tears ran down his cheeks. He was ready to give up. He didn't care anymore.

A sudden wave broke out of the ocean, it crested high, and water rushed over the pier, soaking him. He closed his eyes and held his breath. A familiar sharp pain jabbed at the bottom of his left foot.

Gasping in shock, he rolled onto his side, and everything went dark.

He slowly woke up. Where was he? He felt confused and weak. What happened? Why was he lying on a hard ground? Why wasn't he in bed? Where was his wheelchair? Disoriented, he couldn't figure out where he was. Then he remembered—he was on the pier. He had come here with a desperate hope to be cured.

Dizzy and exhausted, he struggled to sit up. He waited a couple of minutes and then carefully put his shoes back on and pushed himself to his feet. He wished he had brought his wheelchair. The pier looked very long, and he slowly shuffled forward, hoping he could make it all the way back. After what felt like an hour but was probably only a few minutes, weak and shaky, he finally reached the beach and sat on a bench. Holding his face in his hands, he tried to catch his breath and wondered if he would ever feel good again.

After resting about twenty minutes, he slowly stood up and trudged the two blocks home, heavy with worry and fatigue.

Drained and exhausted, he entered his house and collapsed on the couch. He could barely move. All he knew was that he desperately needed to rest, and within moments, he was asleep.

Two hours later, he woke up. Why was he so tired? And why was he on the couch? Memories came back to him. He had walked to the pier and had been jabbed by that creature again. Would it help? Or did that make everything worse?

He sat up. He felt weak and limp. Was he sick again? Or was it the long walk that he was no longer used to? Or was it a result of whatever that creature did to him?

Feeling frail and sluggish, he shuffled to the kitchen. Maybe he simply needed to eat. He grabbed a few things and sat down, staring at the food. Then he ate a hard-boiled egg and some toast, and washed it down with orange juice.

Feeling a bit better but still exhausted and unsteady, he returned to the living room. He slumped down on the couch and quickly dozed off again.

An hour later, he woke up. His mind felt clear and he felt more like his old self. Was he okay? He was afraid to look. He slowly bent forward, pulled down his sock, and inspected his foot. The scaly crust was almost gone. Relieved, he sat back and let out a long breath.

Was he getting better? Was he still ill? He did not know, but he liked feeling more normal again. Sensing he was a little stronger now, he stood up. He felt steadier and healthier than before. Maybe the previous exhaustion was his body recuperating from whatever that was. Maybe he simply needed that downtime to heal and recover. He wasn't sure, but he desperately needed to believe he would be okay.

Whatever happened was out of his control, but he now trusted that the alien entity had tried to help him, and he silently thanked whoever that creature was.

A burst of energy flowed through him, and he stood up and stretched. Not wanting to waste this moment of strength and clarity, he quickly cleaned the kitchen. It actually felt good to move now. Maybe this would be a good day. Maybe he would finally heal.

He might even go back to the pier again tomorrow. Maybe he wouldn't even need the wheelchair. He'd have to see how he felt at that time.

For now, he would hang on to hope.

***

Six months later, Scottie stretched his muscles as he prepared to run. The rain had ended a couple of hours earlier, and he peered out the window. The sun now peeked through the clouds and the ground was beginning to dry. Feeling strong and healthy, he glanced at the wheelchair now pushed into a corner of the room. He had not needed it in a long time.

Shaking his head, he was still amazed at everything that had happened. His mind drifted back to his last medical checkup a few months earlier. The doctor found no trace of the illness that had wracked Scottie's body for so many years. Baffled, the doctor ran the tests one more time, but they again came back negative. Scottie's body had been completely healed and he was free of the disease. The physician stared at him and said he had never seen that happen before, and he made it clear that if any symptoms returned, Scottie should immediately come back for another examination. Scottie assured the doctor he would, but he knew the disease would not come back. He was healed, and he felt strong and healthy.

Now he opened the front door of his house and breathed deeply. The fresh smell of the air after the rain invigorated him. As he started his daily run, he again gave thanks to the unknown alien who had helped him. He had his life back, and he was still in awe.

Feeling energized, he picked up the pace, his shoes slapping rhythmically on the damp ground as he ran. There was so much he did not understand about what happened, but he knew one thing. The world, and what was beyond it, was truly amazing.

Deep joy filled him, and his heart overflowed with gratitude. He knew he would treasure every moment of his life, and he would always be immensely grateful.

~~~

CAUGHT ON FILM

A djusting his camera for a close-up shot, Jeremy squatted and held his breath as he clicked the shutter. Even without his macro lens, he figured that would be a great shot of the bright orange poppies. He took a few more shots at varying angles and distances, stood up, and stretched.

Walking through the field always refreshed and renewed him. Nothing else existed but him and nature and his camera. He inhaled deeply, savoring the fresh fragrance of the native plants and wildflowers that grew there.

As he turned to look for another shot, movement got his attention. Squinting into the distance, he saw a large, round metal object a few hundred yards away, and two beings standing in front of it. Confused and bewildered, he squinted again, trying to see better. *Was that ...*

He sucked in a deep breath and watched. It was clearly some type of alien spacecraft and two alien creatures in front of it. *What the ...*

He watched for a couple minutes as the alien creatures fiddled with a metallic device. Then instinct clicked in. He quickly switched to a telephoto lens, raised his camera, zoomed in, and took pictures. Grateful that it was a new roll of film, he zoomed in even further and clicked away, taking multiple shots of the aliens and the spaceship. A shiver ran up his spine as he realized not only what he was taking pictures of, but that he also needed to get away before he was seen.

Suddenly the aliens stood up straight and peered in his direction. Did they see him? Nervous and jittery, sweat rolling down his back, he crouched down.

His legs felt weak as the aliens took a few steps toward him and raised a strange object, aiming it at him.

Noooooo!

Blackness enveloped him.

A few hours later, Jeremy woke up dazed, flat on his back, groggy, and achy. He was still in the field and the camera was still in his hand. Why was he lying down? Did he lie down for a nap? He couldn't figure it out.

His head pounded with a headache that seemed to get worse by the minute. He slowly sat up and rubbed his temples. His entire body ached. What happened? He couldn't remember anything other than taking pictures of poppies.

He stood up, licked his dry lips, and looked around. Nothing was unusual—a field of grasses, trees, a few bushes, and colorful wildflowers. His mind felt fuzzy and it was hard to concentrate. Why didn't he feel well? Why had he been lying down? It felt like he was missing some crucial bit of information, but he couldn't quite grasp it.

On shaky, rubbery legs, he stumbled back through the field to the parking lot and found his car. Could he drive okay? He thought so—at least he'd be sitting down. He got in his car, grabbed a water bottle, and took a long drink. Feeling a little better, he carefully drove home, his mind trying to figure out what happened. It was like his memory just wasn't there—something was missing, or maybe he was simply overtired.

Once home, he took a couple pills for his headache and then took a deep breath. It was good to be home. Whatever he had taken photos of, he hoped the pictures came out. And maybe that would shed some light on what happened. And if not, at least he'd have some good pictures anyway.

Grateful for having his own darkroom, he entered the room, shut the door, and turned on the red light. After putting on gloves, he carefully removed the film from the camera. He checked the developer, fixer, rinse, chemicals needed, the thermometer, and clips for hanging the film to dry. He was ready. Still feeling a little out of it and somewhat nervous, he started the developing process.

A short time later, he inspected the film. He placed the negatives on a lightbox on his dining room table, grabbed a magnifying glass, and peered at the images.

For some strange reason, a few shots showed that the film was clearly burned in places, and some images were destroyed, and he had no idea why. But most of the images were good. Vivid colors of the poppies greeted his eyes. And then ... what was that? Did someone play a trick on him?

Incredibly clear images were there. Indisputable, crystal clear. Gray-green alien beings, their skin glistening in the sunlight, large black oval eyes, and a metallic device between them. A spaceship behind them. Jeremy gasped as he bent forward, studying the images. Vague memories tickled at the outer fringes of his mind. A shot where the alien beings looked directly at the camera. His eyes opened wide as he studied the last shot: the aliens holding a metallic device, aimed directly at him.

That's what happened! They must have erased my memory! Shaky, hands trembling and eyes wide, he stared at the images. Who could he give these to? Who would believe him? He needed to call the TV news stations, the newspaper, and the police. He had proof, and this would make an incredible story.

Feeling weak, he sat down and rubbed his face. And what if he were asked questions? He couldn't remember anything. It was a shaky story at best. And if no one believed him … this could ruin his career. Was it worth it? A wave of nausea ran through him and he broke out in a sweat.

After taking a few deep breaths, he inspected the images again. He could almost remember … it looked so familiar … he had been there …

He reached for his phone. They may have taken away part of his memory, but he had proof. He had pictures and the original negatives. The story needed to be told.

Suddenly distracted by sizzling and crackling that filled his mind, he put the phone back down. What was happening? Closing his eyes, he held his head in his hands and took deep breaths.

The memories immediately rushed back, clear and vivid. He saw all of it—the spaceship, the creatures, the device … and he could hear a strange buzzing and chirping. *What was that?*

Instantly he understood. He could hear and understand their language. Whatever they shot him with must have opened some channel and created a connection. He knew why they were there and what they wanted. A shudder rushed through him. *They were definitely not friendly.*

He gasped in horror as the realization hit him more forcefully. After harvesting various resources and what they needed from Earth, they wanted to make sure humans did not interfere. They were going to land, invade, and annihilate any humans they encountered. And it would be under the cover of a thunderstorm, which would become widespread.

Who could he tell? He had to warn everyone—or at least somehow get the word out. But this was even less believable than simply seeing alien beings. He would be laughed at and branded a mad man, crazy, insane.

He sat for a few minutes, thinking. As he considered his options, thunder boomed overhead, followed by an intense flash of lightning. Within seconds, another crash of thunder exploded, rattling the windows of his house.

Crackling sounds filled his mind. Jeremy could hear and feel their presence.

They were here. It was happening. Now.

And it was too late.

~~~

LOOSE ENDS

Evan pressed his thumb against the small screen that verified his identity, and the door slid open with a soft whoosh. He quickly strode through, Lucas at his side. After a few more steps, he leaned forward at the next door for the eye scan, and that door slid open, allowing both men to enter the inner sanctum, a large, beige, rectangular room where a few benches were placed in the center, and various alcoves lined the walls. A few locked doors led to various offices and storage areas.

Quickly glancing around, Evan noted the room was empty. That was good. He wasn't expecting anyone here at this hour, and he didn't want any problems. The two agents needed to do this quickly and without any interference.

Evan pointed to one alcove. "That's the one."

Lucas nodded. "Yes, that's it. Let's do this."

They approached the alcove where the special earthenware jug was kept. Although appearing to simply be an artifact used for decoration, it contained a vital link for teleporting. The apparatus they needed for teleporting was inside the jug, and with the programmed device they carried to activate the transport mechanism stored there, they could get where they needed to be. And they needed to get there as soon as possible.

Evan glanced at Lucas. "You ready?"

Lucas nodded. "Yes. It's been way too long already."

Evan tightened his lips. "I agree. It's a rescue long overdue, and I hope they are still alive."

Lucas shook his head. "Those alien creatures must be stopped and prevented from doing this again." He pointed to the jug. "Let's get there. The sooner we get the family out and bring them home, the better. It's eating at me."

Evan peered into the jug and then took a device from his pocket. "All systems are ready."

"Good." Lucas nodded. "Let's go."

Evan activated the device from his pocket and entered the code. He then held the mechanism from the jug, keyed in the data, and verified the accuracy. Then he placed it back in the jug, and they both held the connecting rod.

A familiar whirring noise, a blast of air, and a rush of dizziness enveloped them. Seconds later, they felt a blast of cold air. They stood in a small stone enclosure, the receiving area at Planet Alpha Nirtos 365.

Evan and Lucas remained in the dark enclosure for a few minutes to get their bearings, then slowly emerged, hugging the side of the building and staying in the shadows.

"There." Evan pointed at the long, gray, metallic building. "They're in that building. I remember it from the last time. That's where they do their experiments. It will end today." His breath came out in visible puffs in the frigid air.

Soft sounds of whimpers and sobs reached them. Evan felt his skin crawl and his stomach knot up. Those alien beings were cruel and they had not stopped their brutal and ruthless experiments. He wished they could have come sooner. But he couldn't let himself get distracted by those thoughts. They were here now, and they needed to rescue the endangered family.

Lucas glanced around the landscape, taking in the jagged rocks, red dirt, and strange structures at odd angles in the dimming light. "We came at a good time. Look—the two suns are going down. It will be dark soon. The aliens will rest and sleep, and we can make our move."

Evan let out a long breath and shivered in the cold air. "It's a shame these creatures went against their word and no longer abide by the galactic rules for proper, compassionate, and humane treatment."

"I know. We trusted them. But they do not honor or respect other life forms. And abiding by those rules is critical." Lucas glanced around and rubbed his arms for warmth. "I don't care what they do to their own people, but when they harm other species, they cannot get away with it. They must be stopped."

"I agree. The Council will deal with them. But in the meantime, we must get these people out of here. And when we leave, we will make sure they cannot get any new victims."

A few gray, long-limbed, spindly creatures, covered in a reflective sheen, ambled across the landscape and disappeared.

Darkness slowly fell over the area, and an eerie silence saturated the cold air. An occasional human whine or soft sob could be heard, carried in the thin atmosphere.

Evan tapped Lucas on the arm. "Let's go."

They quietly scurried to the gray building and tried the door. Unlocked. As the beings on this planet had no crime, there was no need to lock the doors.

A long, dark corridor stretched before them, with rooms open on either side. A whimper came from down the hall. The two agents rushed forward toward the sound.

Evan pointed to a room on the left, and they entered the dark room. A small amount of residual light was enough for the two men to see. Three people were restrained on horizontal platforms. A low moan came from the woman on one platform. On another platform, a small child squirmed against the restraints and sobbed. On the third platform, a man took a sharp intake of breath and then released it.

Evan's chest constricted with anguish at seeing their pain and despair. He spoke quietly and urgently. "Please remain quiet. Do not be afraid. We are human. We are here to rescue you. We will not hurt you." He paused. "Are you okay?"

The woman gasped and her voice was raspy. "Please. We are in pain. They keep hurting us. Please help us."

Evan rushed to her side and inspected the clamps. After a brief examination, he realized they were simple to work, and he quickly opened them. "Can you move?" He helped her sit up and held her as she found her balance. She seemed dizzy and woozy.

"I think so." Her voice was weak but desperate.

The two men opened the clamps on the other two platforms, releasing the other humans. Lucas helped the man sit up and Evan went to the child.

The small boy, looking to be around eight years old, looked back at him, his eyes wide with terror and desperation. His face seemed haunted. "Can you help us?" he asked in a small whisper. "I don't like them. I don't like this place."

"Yes," Evan answered. "We will get you out of here. I can carry you if needed." His gut ached as he saw the suffering in the boy's face. "What is your name?"

The boy hesitated, his voice quiet. "Jacob."

"We will help you, Jacob. We will help you and your family."

Evan turned to the woman. "Can you stand on your own? Please try standing. Slowly."

She nodded, slid off the platform, and stood up. Her legs started buckling, but she caught herself and leaned against the platform. Evan reached out and held her arms until she was stable. "Wait here. Don't move."

Evan turned to the man and helped him stand and get his bearings. He appeared weak but okay. "Is there anyone else? Or just you three?"

The man shook his head. "Just us." His voice wavered. "I am Thomas, and my wife is Sylvia. Please help us."

Lucas helped Jacob get down, and the boy quickly ran to his mother and hugged her legs.

Evan looked at the three. "Can you guys walk?" He waited until they nodded. "Please come with us. We will get you out of here."

As they stepped forward, Sylvia stumbled and gasped, and her husband grabbed her and held her. She leaned against him and stifled a sob.

"Please. We must go now." Evan's voice was urgent.

They slowly trudged down the long hallway, and Lucas carefully opened the door and peered outside in the dim light.

Nothing. All was quiet. A gust of cold air blew into the building, and he motioned for everyone to follow.

The two agents helped the family scurry across a barren field. Sylvia, holding her son, stumbled a few times, as Evan held her arm for support and Thomas kept pace at her side. They rushed over a rocky path, and finally arrived at the rock-covered enclosure where the agents had first arrived.

Evan inspected the enclosure. Set into one wall, a panel glowed with various indecipherable inscriptions on them. Evan glanced at Lucas. "We're ending this, right?"

Lucas held his gaze. "Absolutely. Destroy it. It must end now."

Evan nodded grimly and removed a small device from a hidden pocket in his jacket. He quickly attached a small delayed-reaction mini-explosive to the panel. Holding his breath, he made sure it was hooked up properly.

Taking another device from his pocket, Evan entered the codes and then tapped on a few keys, verifying the programming. It was set.

He glanced at the group. "Everyone ready?" They nodded. "Please hold hands—there must be skin contact." The two agents held onto the rod with one hand and grabbed the arms of the injured humans with their other. Evan paused and made sure everyone was connected. "Ready? Don't let go."

Evan pressed *activate* on the explosive device. It would detonate in precisely three minutes.

He then quickly checked the group—everyone was holding hands or touching each other's skin. Evan and Lucas firmly held onto the rod and again verified the family was connected. Evan pressed *start* on the homing device.

An alien shout cut through the air. Alarmed, Evan took in a quick breath, but he knew their group would be gone within seconds. And if the aliens searched the area first, the detonation would go off before they could find it or stop it. Maybe he should have set it for just one minute, but it was too late now.

A familiar whirring noise, a blast of air, and a rush of dizziness enveloped them. Seconds later, they felt a blast of cool air and then the familiar smells of the sanctuary on Earth. They were home.

Evan immediately glanced at the family. Jacob spun around, taking in the surroundings, a combination of fear, relief, and fatigue etched on his face. Sylvia trembled, took a step, and began to fall as her legs gave out and her eyes rolled back in her head. Thomas gasped and reached for her. Evan caught her and laid her gently on the ground.

Thomas quickly kneeled next to his wife and patted her hand. "Sylvia," he called to her. "Sylvia!" He looked up at Evan. "Is she okay?"

Evan nodded. "She should be fine. It's most likely a combination of exhaustion and stress from the travel in addition to whatever they have done to her on that planet." He could feel the man's anguish, and he returned his gaze. "This happens if someone is in a weakened condition and they are not used to this type of travel. It's temporary. She'll be fine."

Lucas opened a small device and scanned the woman's body. "She's okay," he stated. "Just give her a few minutes to recover and get her strength back. I'll go get some water and a blanket."

A rumbling sound came from the jug in the alcove, and Evan turned to it. "I hope that was the panel exploding on their end, and not them coming through."

Lucas came back with a glass of water, a pillow, and a blanket, and crouched next to the woman.

Evan warily approached the jug and looked inside. The device had shifted. He took it out, noting the surprising warmth in his hand, and looked at it. He keyed in the planet they had visited—Alpha Nirtos 365. Two seconds later, it showed an error message: *RECEIVER NOT FOUND. BYPASS RECEIVER AND PROCEED?* He punched "no" and replaced it in the jug.

Letting out his breath, he glanced at Lucas. "We did it. Their panel is destroyed."

Lucas nodded. "And hopefully that means other victims in the galaxy are safe from them. At least for now." He adjusted the blanket on the woman and checked her oxygen reading.

"True." Evan gestured toward the woman. "How is she?"

"She's doing better. She'll be able to leave soon."

"Good. Let's—" A flash of light cut off Evan's words. He glanced at the boy.

Something in the boy's wrist flashed. ***What the* ...** He approached Jacob and pointed to the boy's wrist. "What is that?"

Jacob shrugged. "They put it in me. I don't like it."

Lucas looked up. "It's an implant. They put some type of device in him."

Evan held the boy's arm and watched the light flash. "It's a tracking device. They can locate him."

Lucas nodded. "We have to get that out."

Jacob cocked his head. "Bing. Bing. Bing."

Evan watched him. "What?"

Jacob stared straight ahead. "Bing. Bing. Bing."

"What does that mean?" Evan asked him.

The boy shrugged. "I don't know. I just hear it. I heard it on that planet too. But it's stronger now."

"Is it coming from that planet?"

The boy nodded. "Yes. Bing. Bing. Bop. Bing. Bing. Bop. Blippity. Bing. Bing. Bop."

Evan thought for a few moments. "Is that some kind of code? A language?"

Lucas stood up. "No—it's a familiar sequence. It is probably a mechanism of theirs that connects to various devices such as implants, and it reads them and sends messages. My guess is they are trying to access Jacob's implant."

Evan stared at the flashing light in Jacob's wrist. "Can we neutralize it? Can we stop it from receiving or sending a signal?"

Lucas nodded. "Yes. We can neutralize it and we can also send back a signal that will hopefully scramble their device. Who knows how many others they did this to and how many other implants are out there."

"True. Let's first take care of this one."

Jacob's hand trembled and his eyes brimmed with tears. "Will this hurt?"

Evan stroked Jacob's hair. "No, this won't hurt. You might feel a vibration, that's all. But it won't hurt."

Sylvia coughed, and Lucas helped her sit up. "Are you okay?" He searched her face.

The woman looked around. "Yes, I think so. Just a little dizzy." She waited for a few moments and then struggled to stand up.

Lucas stayed at her side. "Take a few deep breaths," he told her. He led her to one of the benches so she could sit comfortably.

Evan opened a door at the far end of the room, searched through a few drawers, and quickly returned, holding a small apparatus. He motioned to the young boy. "Jacob, come sit here next to me and just relax."

Jacob sat next to him on one of the benches and held out his arm. Evan programmed the device and then held it over Jacob's wrist. As the device buzzed, the light in Jacob's wrist flashed, then sputtered and grew weaker. A gentle hum came from his wrist.

"It's vibrating," the boy said, a touch of fear in his voice.

Evan pressed a few more keys and again held it over Jacob's wrist. The humming sound increased, then abruptly ended. The light gave one weak flash and went dark.

"Hey, it's hot," Jacob said, shaking his wrist.

Lucas rushed over with an ice cube wrapped in a cloth. "Here, put this on it. This will help. The device should now be inactive and won't give you any more trouble." He held the cold cloth over Jacob's wrist. "And we'll remove the implant shortly."

Evan looked around. "We need to get out of here and report in."

Lucas nodded. "And the family needs to be decontaminated and interviewed."

"Wait," Jacob muttered. "I can still hear them."

Evan snapped his head toward the boy. "What?"

Jacob shrugged. "I heard them while we were on their planet. I could hear them in my head. But I just heard them again. Softer, but I heard them."

Lucas stared at the boy, worry etched on his face. "You heard them? Actual words?"

Jacob nodded. "Yeah. Words and impressions of words. Their voices. Their ideas and intentions. Like what they focus on."

Evan glanced at Lucas. "The implant may have opened up a link to them." He crouched next to the boy. "Are you still picking them up? What are they saying?"

"Well, it's weaker now." He scrunched his eyes. "They are upset. They know we are gone. They weren't done with us." He paused. "They want to find other people to replace us." He turned his head to the side as he tuned in. "They don't know what went wrong or how we escaped. They are confused and angry." He bit his lip and swallowed. "Wait. They found the panel. It is destroyed. They are now searching for a backup device. They have a few of them."

Sylvia gasped and Evan turned to her. "Are you okay?"

The woman held out her arm. A light flashed in her wrist. "I have one too," she said, barely audible.

Evan turned to Lucas. "We need to scan them for additional implants. Thomas probably has one too, and there may be more than one implant in each of them."

Lucas pursed his lips. "Let's get to work. We have a lot to do."

Sylvia picked up Jacob and held him. "We're ready. Whatever it takes."

Thomas stood next to her. "Yes. We'll do anything we can to help."

Evan gestured toward them. "Good. Then let's get going. We're going to end this and block any connection they have to you." He shook his head. "It's going to be a busy day."

~~~

WHITE STUFF

C aptain **Harris Miles Stanbury** surveyed the planet's landscape through the main viewscreen as a rush of adrenaline moved through him. He loved being the captain and he especially loved exploring new worlds. The excitement, the thrill, the danger, and the rewards were enormous.

After receiving a communication signal from Captain Marshall from the planet's surface a month earlier about the incredible discovery on this planet, that it was "better than gold," he had to come take a look for himself. He knew Captain Marshall from the Academy, and they had shared with each other reports from other space explorations. Harris had not heard from him since then, but he knew he was a good captain and he trusted him. He felt the excitement rise and couldn't wait to get down on the planet's surface to see what was there.

Exciting possibilities rushed through his mind now that he was finally in orbit, ready to explore this magnificent world. What was down there? What was "better than gold"? He couldn't wait to set foot on the surface.

Looking through the main viewscreen, his gaze took in the red and brown dirt, rocks, and a few strange, elongated, green-tinged objects. He would need to see what those were. And it looked like a few patches of white material were sprinkled over some of the ground. Maybe that's what Captain Marshall was talking about. He would make sure they collected some of that white stuff.

After calling his crew together, he looked at each person before addressing them. "Although we have determined that the air is breathable and not toxic, we will all wear full spacesuits to make sure there is no contamination. I will take six of you down to the surface with me for exploration and collection of samples."

He pointed to six of the crew as he continued. "Spencer, Garrett, Tyson, Wade, Lucas, and Kendra, you're coming down with me. Suit up and meet me in Shuttle Bay One in twenty minutes. The rest of you," he added, nodding to the others, "will remain here on standby for further orders."

Adrenaline coursed through him. He lived for these explorations and discoveries.

***

The captain stepped onto the ground, feeling as excited as a kid. The thrill of setting foot on a new planet never got old. Each new exploration was as exciting as the first time. Harris scanned the area. His crew was good and knew what they were doing. He trusted them.

After watching them spread out and start collecting samples, he wandered over to a patch of the white material sprinkled over the ground. What was that? His gloved hand pushed it around. It felt a bit powdery and sandy, but he couldn't tell what it was. They would examine the samples later, and he looked forward to receiving the answer. He stood up and continued walking.

The dirt and rocks looked ordinary. He peered at one of the long, curved, green-tinged objects. Goosebumps rose on his arms, and something told him not to touch it. He watched it for a couple minutes, simply observing. He thought he detected a slight movement, but he wasn't sure. Did he imagine it? He stepped back. They had not detected any life forms on this planet, and if this thing was alive, then it was something completely unknown.

102

It could be a life form they knew nothing about, and he did not want any confrontations, injuries, or problems.

He stepped away and his gaze searched the area. What had Captain Marshall referred to? What was so valuable? He couldn't see anything on this planet that seemed worthy, and he headed back to his crew.

Of the six who had come to the surface, only three were now visible. Where were the other three? He felt a lump form in his throat. Something was wrong. A tremor of fear ran up his spine.

New mounds of white stuff were piled where the crew had been earlier. Where did those come from? His hair stood on end.

"Garrett! Tyson! Kendra!" he called out. "Where are the others?"

The three crew members turned and looked around, scanning the area. The captain's eyes searched the area too, as worry crept into his belly. Something was definitely not right. His belly churned with anxiety. What was happening?

After looking in all directions, he glanced back to the three crew members. Only Kendra now remained. Where were the other two? Terror raced up his spine. "Kendra!" he called to her.

Kendra stood frozen in place, and through her face plate, the captain could see bafflement and fear on her face.

New piles of white stuff now covered the area. What was that stuff? It had not come from the air. Could it have come from the ground? And where was his crew? What was happening? Why were they disappearing? He shivered with fear.

Gesturing to Kendra, he was about to say something when she blinked out of existence. A pile of white stuff now occupied the space where she had stood moments before.

What the—

Overwhelming terror gripped him. They needed to get out of there. *Now!*

As he turned toward the shuttle, the remainder of his crew from the spaceship suddenly appeared on the planet, and none of them wore spacesuits. Panic swept over him—how was this possible? Their faces registered shock, and he could not comprehend what was happening. Why were they down on the surface? They knew to remain on the ship and wait for instructions.

The crew then instantly disappeared, as mounds of fresh white stuff covered the ground where they had been standing.

Something was horribly wrong, and the captain started to rush toward the shuttle.

After two steps, everything went black.

***

A pile of white stuff remained behind where the captain had been.

A communication signal was sent across space, in Captain Harris Miles Stanbury's voice. *"Wow, you need to come here to this planet! This is amazing—an incredible discovery! It is better than gold! Come look!"*

One elongated, green-tinged creature slithered to the white stuff and began ingesting the new tasty morsels. Three hundred more creatures came forward, glided over, and enthusiastically joined in the feast.

<p style="text-align:center">~~~</p>

STEPPING OUT OF TIME

S tanding in her den, Carla admired the beautiful water jug which she had picked up at a garage sale a few months earlier. Something had immediately drawn her to it, and it now sat in an alcove in the wall at her home in San Francisco. Looking at it, she smiled. It was one of her favorite finds from a garage sale.

Stepping forward, she reached for the jug, a beautiful artifact from long-ago days. As her fingers grazed across the surface, she felt a vibration, almost a shock. *What was that?* Pulling her arm back, she stared at it. Then she gingerly reached for it again and rested her palm against it, feeling a low vibration and hearing a humming sound.

Curious, she grabbed it and lifted it up, admiring the hefty weight of the jug. Looking inside it, she wondered who used it and how it had been used.

She was suddenly in a busy market on a dusty dirt field, and she blinked in the bright sunlight. Many people walked through the market and stopped at various stalls. The voices of sellers calling out their wares permeated the air. Women wearing rags bargained for lower prices for food and items they needed.

"Are you gonna buy that?" a man's voice addressed her.

"What?" Carla looked up.

"The jug. It's my best selling item. Do you want it or not?"

Shocked, she put it back down on the table in front of her, along with the other pottery items. "Um, no, sorry, not today."

As she released the jug and pulled her fingers back, she found herself again in the den of her home in San Francisco, staring at the jug in the alcove.

Her mouth dry, she stared in disbelief. *What just happened?* It sure seemed like she had been transported to another time and space, but that was impossible ... Maybe it was just a daydream or a hallucination.

Her fingers trembling slightly, she slowly reached forward and touched the jug again.

She was immediately back in the busy market, voices calling out, dust swirling around.

The seller stared at her. "Well, make up your mind. Either buy it or not."

Carla gasped. "I ... I'm sorry." She removed her hand from the jug and was instantly back in her den at home.

She swallowed hard, a knot forming in her belly. It made no sense. Backing up, she stared at the jug. Goosebumps rose on her arms. She shook her head and turned away.

Feeling spooked, she went into the kitchen and made a cup of tea and sat down, trying to relax. By the time she finished the warm, soothing drink, she found herself intrigued. She needed to know what was happening with that artifact.

Walking back into the den, she glanced at the jug. It was beautiful and had clearly been used a lot in its heyday. Feeling drawn to it, she slowly approached it and reached toward it. Her hands shaking, she grasped the handle.

Instantly, she was back in the busy market, facing the man behind the table.

"Well?" He glared at her.

"Okay," she said. "I'll buy it. How much?"

After she paid the man, she held the jug against her body and left the market, walking along a dirt road. Turning around, she looked back at the hustle and bustle of the people buying and selling food and other items. It looked strange but also somehow felt familiar.

"Bethany, there you are. How are you doing?" A warm female voice interrupted her thoughts, and Carla turned to see a middle-aged woman, her brown hair in a tight bun, smiling at her.

Somehow Carla knew this woman and her name came to her right away. "Tillie, it's nice to see you here." How did she remember the name? "Look what I got." Carla, now Bethany, held up the jug.

Tillie smiled. "You've had your eye on that for a while now. I'm glad you finally got it."

"Yes, it was time. I really wanted it." She felt nervous trying to keep up a conversation. Who was this Tillie? She knew it was someone she was close to, but she couldn't quite remember who, and she didn't want to say anything wrong.

Tillie laughed. "Well, it will come in handy. We can always use another one." She smiled wider, showing a gap where a tooth was missing. "We need to get back and start fixing something for supper. I thought you could make that stew we love that you make so well."

"Oh yes, I love that stew," Bethany answered quickly. "I'll start making that."

"Good. Well, I need to pick up more potatoes first. You run on home, and I'll be there shortly to help."

"Okay." Bethany watched Tillie head into the market, her long skirt swishing behind her. She glanced down and saw she was wearing a similar long skirt. Where were they? Who were they? And when was this?

Anxiety churned in her belly. She wanted to be back home. She placed the jug on the ground and let go. Nothing happened. She was still there on the dusty road just outside the market.

Worry gripped her. How was she supposed to get back to her own time and place? What if she couldn't get back? Tears burned her eyes. She had no idea what to do. Was she stuck here now?

Shaking her head, she looked around, shielding her eyes with her hand against the midday sun.

She was suddenly back in her den in her modern home. Gasping, she quickly pulled her hand back from the jug. Her eyes widened as horror filled her. Vowing never to touch the jug again, she slowly backed out of the room.

Vague memories flitted through her mind. Tillie had been her sister. She remembered her more clearly now. They were close, and she loved Tillie. But that was another lifetime, a past life suddenly in the present. It felt so real—she was right there in it again. The sounds, the sights, the smells—she was *there*. This jug somehow linked her to that previous lifetime. Was it the same jug? And even if it were, how was any of this possible?

Wanting to have nothing more to do with the jug, she stayed out of the den the rest of the day.

The following day, many questions still churned in her mind. And part of her longed for her sister. She loved and worried about Tillie. She was drawn back to the den, staring at the jug with wide eyes. She was sure it was the same jug.

Without thinking, she found herself walking toward it, her hand outstretched. Before she could stop herself, she grabbed the handle of the jug.

Instantly, she was back on the dusty road. She watched Tillie walk into the market toward the man with the potatoes they liked. She felt herself smile. The stew would be good—it was her favorite meal to make. Turning, she headed off down the dirt path toward home. Maybe she would add peas and carrots and onions to the stew. She hoped they had some pork to add in, but they didn't always have enough.

Wait! What was she doing? This was not her time. This was the past. She didn't belong here. She was Carla, not Bethany. She put the jug back on the ground and stood there, hoping to return to San Francisco. Nothing happened. She remained on the dirt path. She was still Bethany, somehow now stuck in a past life.

Standing there for ten minutes, she hoped it would wear off and she would return to her normal time. Nothing changed. As a few people passed by, she waved and smiled at them. Finally, she picked up the jug and headed toward home.

After walking about thirty minutes, she turned down a small path and found herself facing a small hut, and she knew this was her home. She slowly opened the front door and went into the dimly lit interior. A few old, worn, but comfortable sofas were arranged in the middle of the room. Memories of family and celebrations flooded her. Turning to the right, she headed into the kitchen. A large wooden table took up the back part of the room.

She smiled as images came to her of happy times at family meals with everyone talking at once.

It was time to start the stew. Bethany gathered the vegetables and brought them to a small counter and started chopping them. She would make the stew she was famous for, and she would make it even better this time. Tillie would love it, and she smiled as she worked.

As she turned to grab another carrot, something fell to the floor. Stooping down, she picked it up. A photograph. At first she did not recognize the futuristic woman in the photo. Someone dressed in strange clothes, but still familiar ...

Goosebumps suddenly rose on her from head to toe. That woman in the photo ... a face she knew. But how was this possible? She stared at the image again—it was *her!* Her belly quivered. It was her from the future! But how could she even know that ...

Her gaze was drawn to the jug that sat on the counter. That was the link. But why would she have a picture from the future?

It suddenly hit her. She was now stuck in the past. She had a different life somewhere. But how could she get back? Was she now stuck here in a past life permanently?

She looked back at the photo. Her familiar, smiling face looked back at her. A face from a life she was supposed to be living now. But ... but she now had the stew to make. Tillie was counting on her to make it.

She held the photo to her chest and closed her eyes.

When she opened them, she was back in her den in San Francisco. She was home.

She glanced at the jug. A note was now firmly attached to the front of it, and she leaned closer to read it.

I had to send something to you from this time period—a lifeline—to bring you back. Do not go back there again. You will be stuck there and I will not be able to bring you home again.

Carla stared at it as a sob welled up in her chest. But what would happen with the stew ... her heart was torn ... She put her hands down to grasp her long skirt, but it was no longer there. She was now wearing jeans.

Confused and overwhelmed, she looked around her modern apartment. No, she didn't belong back in the past anymore. That was a past life, and she had already lived that. She needed to remain in the present. She was Carla again, not Bethany, and she needed to stay here.

She ran to the hall closet, searched on the shelves, and picked up a hammer. Then she rushed back to the den, and before she could change her mind, she brought it down hard on the jug, smashing it into pieces. She would throw it out later.

A choking sob rose in her chest as her heart ached for Tillie, her sister, who she now deeply missed. She glanced at the shards of pottery now sitting in the alcove.

"I hope you liked the stew, Tillie," she whispered, as one tear slowly slid down her cheek.

~~~

MESSAGE DECIPHERED

H olding his wife's hand, Bruce gazed thoughtfully at the fascinating display of Stonehenge in front of them. It was a powerful moment seeing it in person.

After a few minutes, he looked around and gazed up into the blue sky above them. Suddenly Bruce gasped and pointed. "Oh no!"

Wanda glanced at him. "What?" Her gaze followed his finger, and her eyes widened as she took in the glowing object streaking across the sky and hurtling toward Earth.

"Look. They are finally doing it." He nervously licked his lips. "They want to wipe us out."

Wanda's brow furrowed. "Who? What do you mean? I don't follow."

Bruce let out a long sigh. "It's a long story. We finally figured out what the stones here at Stonehenge meant. What the configuration was saying." He paused and shook his head. "It was a code planted by aliens long ago."

"And? I don't follow."

Bruce pursed his lips, wondering how much he should tell her. Would it even matter any longer?

"It was a communication to other aliens and a warning to humans. It consisted of three parts." He hesitated and then continued. "One part was directions for how to obtain proper specimens. And the second part—"

"Wait. Proper specimens?"

"Yes—directions for other alien beings who come here. How to abduct us, what to take from us, and then how to put us back without our memory of it."

Wanda stared at him for a few moments. "What are they taking from us?"

His voice was soft. "Cells from our brain stem. This communication is a guide saying to systematically take us, test us, analyze us, and take cells from our brain stem." He held her gaze. "The cells are being used as medicine on their world. That's why we were planted here. We are a breeding ground of medicine for them."

She shook her head and her voice came out in a whisper. "How do you know this?"

"I have been working with a group that has extensively studied this along with other alien communications. We have found other messages from them as well." He paused for a moment, considering his words. "We have been studying this for a long time, and we have finally deciphered them."

Her voice was weak. "And there's more to this message?"

"Yes. The second part explains that if we either resist or our cells change, we will no longer be useful, and they will eradicate us. Wipe us out and start over."

Wanda swallowed hard. "And ... and the third part?"

"The third part is a timeline. A date."

A pause. "What date?"

"The closest we could figure was this year, this month."

The horror of his words soaked into her. "And you think ..."

Her words were wiped out by a blinding light and the roar of a device entering the atmosphere.

~~~

Outpost 391

Captain **William Jacobs** tapped his foot and then strode across the bridge and stopped in front of his navigator.

"Marcus, how soon will we be at Outpost 391?"

The navigator looked up. "In forty minutes, Captain. It should be clear sailing the rest of the way."

"Good." Feeling a little on edge, the captain paced back and forth a few times. "When we get there, I don't want to spend too long on the surface of this planet. One hour at the most. It is known to have violent winds that can be dangerous."

"Yes, Captain."

The captain peered out the front viewport. "I don't think this planet will be good for an outpost, but we have orders to check it out, so we need to at least put in the effort. But I want it to be fast—I want to land, take our samples and measurements quickly, and leave. And Marcus, I want you down there with me as part of the landing party."

"Yes, Captain." Marcus pursed his lips. "What about the previous crew who landed there? Do we know what happened to them or what they found?"

William Jacobs shook his head and waved his hand dismissively. "I doubt that ever happened, Marcus. We have no documentation that the crew ever even reached this world, much less landed there. They were sent to check on this planet as a potential outpost, but we never heard from them again. No reports, no contact, nothing after that. So now it's our turn."

Marcus shrugged. "Well, the scuttlebutt says they were killed there while calling for help."

The captain harrumphed. "Killed by what? There are no known life forms on that planet. And there is no evidence that the crew from that ship ever actually landed there or encountered anything. It's all unsubstantiated rumors." He crossed his arms. "It's possible that they were lost and never even made it, or maybe they crash landed. We don't know. Maybe we'll find something when we get there that can answer that."

"Well, the rumors I heard said that—"

"Forget the rumors. We go by facts. We land, take measurements, briefly scout the area to give feedback on its potential use as an outpost, collect a few samples of the soil and rocks, update our data, and we leave. That's it." He paused. He did not want to be sidetracked with needless fears or worries. "I don't want to hear more about unverified rumors. Let's just do our job and get out of there." Already feeling a bit uneasy about this job, he didn't want to dwell on anything that could make it worse.

"Yes, Captain." Marcus faced forward again and checked the readouts on his panel, noting the heading, speed, and other indicators.

The captain reviewed his orders and notes about what was known of the planet that had an area on it known as Outpost 391. Scanning the information for this sector of the galaxy, he looked for anything that could be a potential problem. He prided himself on being efficient and leading his crew on these excursions. He wanted to get the job done as quickly as possible without any incidents, and then report back to his superior. If this was successful, he might even move up in rank. He didn't want any problems or any incidents that could hurt that.

"Captain?" Marcus interrupted his thoughts. "We're approaching the outer atmosphere of the planet now. We'll be in shuttle range in ten minutes."

"Good. Stabilize the orbit, and then we'll meet to review what we need to do on the surface and what we need to take with us."

The navigator nodded. "Yes, Captain."

"I've also asked Edmund join us as part of the landing party. He's a good systems engineer and is excellent with the equipment that we'll need, and he can assist us down there."

"Edmund? He's not the easiest person to—"

"Marcus, that's enough. Hold your comments to yourself for now. I know he may be difficult at times, but he is a genius with that equipment, and we need him. And Marcus," he added, "I expect you to be professional and respectful to him at all times."

"Understood, Captain." Marcus rolled his eyes and then pressed a few buttons. He glanced at the monitor and looked up. "Ready, Captain. Orbit is stable and locked. We can have our meeting and board the shuttle any time now."

"Excellent. Please have the relief navigator cover the bridge while we're gone."

"He's on his way now. Will it be just us three down there?"

The captain nodded. "Yes. I don't want more of my crew down on the surface on this one. I don't expect to be there long, and I want to keep this tight and quick. Let's meet in the conference room in five minutes, review the details, make sure everything is clear, and then we'll go down to the planet and do what's needed."

"Yes, sir. And my relief is here and ready, Captain." Marcus stood up as Kurt entered the bridge to relieve him.

"Good. Let's get going."

***

Marcus guided the shuttle down to the planet's surface. The captain monitored the descent and looked at the readouts, and then he watched the view from the front viewport. Something bothered him about this job and made him nervous, but he wasn't sure what. He just knew that he wanted to get this assignment over with quickly and move on.

Edmund fidgeted in his seat. He glanced out the viewport as he held onto his device.

The captain glanced at Edmund, who was making last-minute adjustments to the controls on the bulky equipment on his lap. "Edmund, how is the equipment? Ready to go?"

The systems engineer looked up. "Yes, Captain. All ready. I'm glad I'm here for this. The inductance node has been sticking and giving incorrect data. But I know this coupling differentiator inside out. With my experience, I know I can adjust it as needed, so we'll be fine."

The captain nodded. "Good. That's why you're here."

Edmund guffawed. "Good thing, too. No one else can do what I can with this. And I hope I won't have to use what I recently discovered with this device, but it can also be used as a weapon."

"That won't be necessary. There are no life forms on this planet."

"Well, just in case, I got your back."

"Okay, Edmund, that's good to know."

A reddish dust cloud enveloped them and blocked their view as the shuttle descended the final one hundred feet and thumped onto the surface.

"I can't see anything," Marcus mumbled, as he fiddled with the controls. He felt the shuttle shudder from a windy blast, and the reddish dust particles dissipated and were swept away.

"Look at that," Edmund said, pointing at the view. "I can't wait to get out there."

The captain peered through the front viewport and surveyed the reddish dirt and barren landscape. A few craters, a few hills, and a group of large boulders to the left were the only objects in their view. The scene was desolate.

He nodded to the two men. "Okay, let's move."

After entering the airlock chamber, they shut the doors and checked their suits and all necessary equipment. Each man carefully put on his spacesuit and adjusted the gear and settings. All oxygen lines were double-checked to make sure everything was functioning properly.

"Suit videos working?" the captain asked both officers.

"Yes, Captain," Marcus responded. "Everything is being recorded."

"Me too, Captain," Edmund said. "Video is working."

"Good. Let's go. And remember—one hour tops, less if we're done sooner. I don't want to be here long."

Marcus nodded. "Got it, Captain."

Edmund looked up from the equipment he was holding. "Yes, Captain. I'm ready."

The captain rechecked and verified all the settings on each suit as another blast of wind shook the shuttle. "Everything looks good," he said as he nodded. "You both clear on what you're doing? Marcus, you record everything and collect samples. Edmund, you work the equipment and get all the readings, measurements, and data that we need. You both know what to do. I will inspect those boulders and see what's behind them and keep an eye on everything. We stay within fifty feet of each other at all times and we don't go beyond two hundred feet of the shuttle. Understood?"

"Yes, Captain," both Marcus and Edmund replied in unison.

Another strong wind jolted the shuttle.

The navigator hesitated. "Captain, that wind is worrying me."

The captain pursed his lips. "I'm concerned too." An uneasiness settled in his belly. He knew he was responsible for his men and the whole mission. He did not want to put them at any unnecessary risk. After thinking for a minute, he gestured toward the supplies. "Let's link up. Get the cable and let's all stay tethered together. I don't want to lose anyone."

"Yes, Captain." Marcus unhitched the cable and brought it to Captain Jacobs. "Is this what you want?"

"Yes, thank you, Marcus." After securing the cable to each of the men, the captain did a final check of all readings on their suits. "Looks good. Okay, let's go."

Marcus hit the buttons regulating air pressure, gravity, oxygen, and temperature, waited for the light to come on, and then opened the door to the outside. A strong wind blew red dust particles across the landscape and then died down.

They eased down the few steps to the planet's surface. Red dirt stretched out in all directions. A small swirl of red dust drifted by and then dissipated.

The captain looked at Marcus and Edmund. "Okay guys, do your thing. Let me know if there are any problems."

They walked forward on the red dirt, stepping away from the shuttle. William Jacobs watched Marcus and Edmund move farther away as they concentrated on their duties. About sixty feet from the shuttle, Marcus squatted and started collecting dirt samples. Edmund fiddled with his device. William was proud of them—they were good officers, efficient and competent, each in his own way, and he was glad they were part of his crew.

The captain nodded, satisfied, and then he headed to the left toward the group of large boulders about forty feet off to the side. A sense of discomfort flooded through him. He shook his head, figuring it was just nerves for being on a new world. This should not take long, and he would be glad when they were back on the ship and leaving. He rounded the first boulder and noticed a small cave between two of the boulders, resembling a shelter. He slowly approached the dark opening as a shiver ran through him.

Once his eyes adjusted to the dim light in the cramped cave, he saw what looked like a narrow table that had been assembled and a rock in front of it which could be used as a seat. It struck him as a deliberate setting. Was there something intelligent here that arranged this? Had the former crew actually made it here? He moved closer for a better look.

His eyes widened as he gasped and stepped back. *No!*

A small spiral notebook, covered with a thick layer of reddish dust, sat at the back of the makeshift table. White dusty bones lay on the floor against one wall of the cave. Human bones.

The captain's throat was dry. He licked his lips and felt weak. It wasn't a rumor after all. The previous team did land here. What happened to the crew? Why didn't they report in?

He slowly reached forward and picked up the notebook. Why had they not sent a message? What happened here? He opened the notebook and saw a short paragraph of scribbled writing on the first page. He began reading.

> *Arrived two hours ago. Waiting for my crew to finish collecting data and samples. This is a windy and barren wasteland. Nothing here. I will investigate further, but I doubt this will work as an outpost. Will send a report shortly. Just want to first make a few notes and check one more thing. I now hear movement outside. Something is not right. I hear something strange out there. A loud roar. What is that? I do not have a weapon with me, as I didn't think there was any life here. But I distinctly hear some type of animal out there. I will check it out and report what I—*

That was the only entry. The human bones, and what looked like old blood stains in the dirt, told the rest of the story. The crew did arrive here. And this officer clearly did not die from natural causes. He was killed before he even sent his first message.

The captain knew his suit-cam was recording everything he saw, and he deliberately turned in a circle to record everything.

A jolt of fear moved through him. If there was an unknown, deadly life form here, they could not stay—they needed to leave immediately. He took the notebook and turned to leave. He would not put his crew in danger—their lives were more important than any data collection. He could hear the wind picking up and then it was quiet again.

Marcus's voice abruptly came through the speaker in his headgear, interrupting his thoughts. "Uh, Captain, we have a problem."

The captain felt his anxiety rise. "On my way."

A loud roar suddenly filled the air.

William felt goosebumps rise on his arms. His stomach lurched. They had to get off this planet—*now*. He hoped it was not too late.

He cautiously peered out from the cave. Nothing. He stealthily exited, hugging the boulders. As he came around into the open, his eyes took in the scene. An enormous, gray, fifteen-foot-tall, rat-like creature, its back toward him, stood between him and his two officers.

The captain observed the scaly skin and obvious strength of the behemoth creature. He knew this creature could easily kill them all. He shivered, thinking of what he had seen in the small cave. Glancing at Marcus and Edmund, thirty feet away from him, he noted their wide eyes and shocked, pale faces through the headgear.

Pointy ears on the massive creature stood upright, as though on alert. It sensed movement behind it and turned toward him. Its yellow eyes looked cold and menacing. It opened its mouth and hissed, revealing razor-sharp teeth that dripped saliva which sizzled as it hit the dirt. It turned back to the other two officers. The captain slowly walked in a wide circle to his left to get around the creature and back to his men.

They were still tethered together. Were they trapped? Were they sitting ducks for this creature? They needed to get to the shuttle—sixty feet away, which looked like a huge distance to cover.

The gargantuan creature squinted its eyes, hissed, then scurried away from them and disappeared down an opening in the ground surrounded by a ring of dirt.

Taking a deep breath, William quickly scanned the area and now noticed more similar holes surrounded by rings of dirt. Were they openings to nests of more creatures? Openings to a network of tunnels below ground? Who knew how many more of these creatures were here. They needed to move out immediately.

"Are you two okay?" William called to his men. They nodded, and he pressed on. "We need to leave. Immediately. Back to the shuttle—both of you. Now."

"Yes," Marcus answered, turning toward the shuttle. "Let's get out of here." He gestured, his arms wide, as they started walking back to the shuttle. "That was huge! Like a gigantic, two-thousand-pound, scaly rat."

Edmund fiddled with the coupling differentiator and then looked up. "It looked like an enormous dinosaur rodent. It had—"

ROOAAAAR!

The captain turned around, tense and alert. The creature was back. A massive rodent covered with dark gray scales stood in front of the hole in the ground. The creature roared again—a guttural, angry scream that reverberated in the thin atmosphere.

The captain felt the hairs rise on his neck, and he stepped back in terror. His muscles tensed. They were still at least fifty feet from the shuttle. Frantic, he looked around for a weapon or anything to hide behind. Nothing.

The three men slowly backed toward the shuttle, keeping their eyes on the creature.

The massive rodent roared again. Its sharp teeth dripped saliva which sizzled on the ground, and its ears pointed forward. Its yellow eyes squinted as it surveyed the three men. A guttural screech filled the air as it opened its mouth. It suddenly reared up and then charged.

The creature raced toward Marcus, whose face contorted in complete horror, his mouth open in a silent scream, as he stumbled backward.

Edmund gripped his machine and quickly ran in the opposite direction, away from them. *What was he doing?* He was moving *away* from the shuttle! *What the hell?*

The creature stopped and looked at Edmund who was now off to the side. The creature roared again and then turned back toward William and Marcus.

Marcus turned and raced toward the shuttle. Still forty feet away from the shuttle, the cable connecting him to Edmund grew taut, jerked, and knocked Marcus off his feet. He fell to the ground, panting with fear. Terror gripped him as he struggled to get up.

The taut cable yanked Edmund and threw him off balance. He stumbled and crashed to the ground. The impact jarred him, but he clutched tightly to the equipment, protecting it as best he could.

The creature lumbered forward, eyeing each of the men.

"Get up, get up!" the captain shouted.

Edmund fiddled with the instrument.

"Edmund, what are you doing?" William yelled. "We need to leave!"

The captain scurried toward Marcus. He glanced at Edmund and saw him kneeling on the ground, still fiddling with the apparatus. "Edmund, move! Come on! Let's go!"

Edmund glanced up. "Trust me, Captain." He focused on the instrument again. "I have to do this. It's our only chance."

Marcus released the cable from his suit to free himself from being tethered, and he continued backing up toward the shuttle. William slowly followed, keeping his eyes on the creature.

The mammoth rat creature hissed, as saliva dripped onto the dirt and sizzled. It threw back its head and roared, a deep, powerful sound. Panic surged through William's body, almost paralyzing him.

The captain raised his voice. "Edmund, let's go. Let's get back to the shuttle. Now!"

The rodent rushed at Marcus.

"NOOOO!" The navigator shrieked and covered his face with his arms. The creature was quickly closing the distance.

The captain desperately looked around for anything he could use as a weapon. He was responsible for his men and he needed to do something to help them and protect them. He would not stand by and watch them die. He picked up a small rock and threw it at the creature. It landed three feet away from it, and the creature twitched at the sound and came to a stop. It hissed, its eyes blazing with malice.

William glanced at Edmund and saw him crouched and aiming the differentiator toward the creature. *What was he doing?*

The immense rat creature now focused on the captain. It squinted its eyes and began slowly lumbering toward him as though stalking its prey. It stopped twenty feet away from him. The captain watched it, his body shaking and pulsing with fear. He was supposed to lead his men, but what could he do?

He felt helpless. He had no weapon. His heart thudded furiously in his chest and his mouth was dry. Were they going to die here? The creature was too close to them and they could not outrun it. There was no way they could get to the shuttle in time.

William took a few steps back. A roar filled the air as the gargantuan rat creature's mouth opened, showing its incredibly sharp teeth. The creature rose up on its hind legs and charged again, now fixated on the captain.

The captain's eyes widened in absolute terror. Fifteen feet away ... ten feet ... six feet ... The creature was almost at him, its mouth open ... It suddenly shrieked and stopped.

William swallowed and quickly ran around the creature, toward Marcus and the shuttle. What happened? And why wasn't Edmund coming? What was he doing? Edmund was still squatting in the red soil, the machine aimed at the creature.

The enormous rat creature turned and hissed angrily at Edmund. Then it focused on Edmund and began creeping toward him. Edmund gasped and furiously punched various controls on the apparatus. A beam shot out and hit the rat creature. The creature shrieked and stopped. It looked stunned. It stood there and hissed and glared at Edmund, but it didn't move.

Edmund stood up and slowly eased closer to Marcus and the captain. "Get in the shuttle," Edmund yelled at the two men. "Now."

The captain waved his arm. "Edmund, I will not leave you—"

129

"Now, dammit!" Edmund fired his instrument at the creature again. The creature roared and started coming forward. Edmund fired again. The creature screeched and stopped, then stood there looking dazed.

The three men raced toward the shuttle. Twenty feet away. They rushed forward. Marcus tripped and then caught himself as William grabbed his elbow in support. Finally five feet from the shuttle, they rushed forward as another roar filled the air.

Breathing heavily, the captain glanced back and saw three more gargantuan rat creatures charging toward them. "Everyone in! Now!" His heart pounded in his chest.

Marcus, Edmund, and the captain rushed up the steps and into the shuttle, quickly closing and locking the door behind them. Marcus nervously fiddled with controls on the wall panel as the small room regulated pressure, oxygen, temperature, and gravity. Their heavy breathing was audible as the shuttle shook. They fidgeted and waited for what seemed like endless minutes as pounding on the door intensified. The green light finally came on, and they quickly took off their spacesuits.

The shuttle rocked. The creatures were out there, forcefully pummeling the spacecraft. Opening the door to the main cabin, the crew rushed in, and the captain glanced out the viewport. Five of those humongous creatures now surrounded the shuttle, scratching at it, rattling the door, and pushing at it.

"Marcus! Take off! Get us out of here!"

The shuttle rocked and then tilted, settling into the ground at an angle.

"What was that? What happened?" Fear flooded through the captain.

Marcus wiped sweat off his brow. "One of the landing legs must have buckled. It was probably damaged by those creatures."

"Take off! Now!" The captain felt sweat dripping down his neck.

"Working on it, Captain. Lift off in thirty seconds."

"Now!" He could not keep the desperation out of his voice.

"Getting all systems up and ready, Captain."

The shuttle shook. A huge thump jarred the door—a powerful force from the outside. Those creatures were incredibly strong. The wind howled. The roar of the creatures filled the air. Those beasts were not giving up.

Marcus looked up. "Twenty more seconds, Captain."

Through the front viewport they now saw over ten creatures swarming the area, roaring, throwing themselves at the shuttle, baring their sharp teeth.

Edmund put down his machine. "I can help, Captain. I can reverse the charge of the electric polarization of the capacitor, and change the resistance so that a voltage is generated between the crystals in the diode ray. It creates a pulse wave with a static charge which can be amplified, and it will jolt them and—"

"Do it!" the captain shouted, spit flying out of his mouth.

Edmund sat next to Marcus, his fingers frantically punching buttons on the control panel. The shuttle vibrated and a loud hum filled the bridge. The creatures outside shrieked and then roared.

"Get us out of here, Marcus."

"Lifting off now."

The shuttle rumbled. The captain felt the familiar heaviness as he sank into his seat while the shuttle lifted.

He leaned forward and looked out the front viewport. There were now more than twenty creatures swarming the area where they had just been.

The shuttle rose, gaining in speed and altitude.

The captain let out his breath. "We would not have survived much longer."

Marcus nodded and licked his lips. "I know, Captain. We barely left in time."

William turned to his systems engineer. "Edmund, why did you run the other way out there? What were you thinking? That delayed us from leaving. We could have—"

"Captain, I needed to split us up to confuse and distract him and buy us a little time to get an advantage. That was all I needed to get the instrument ready. He would have rushed us and killed us all without that extra minute."

William nodded. "That is very possible. But what did you do with that device?"

Edmund grinned. "Well, based on my extensive experience in the intricacies of this differentiator, I simply reversed the polarity of the electron flow in the anode which then—"

"Could you skip that part and get to what it actually did to the creature?"

Edmund chuckled. "It injured him and affected his internal body systems and weakened him, even if only temporarily. It effectively slowed him down. If you noticed, he didn't charge us for a while after that. It bought us more time, which we needed. Otherwise, we would not have made it to the shuttle in time. When he was strong and feeling good, he was much faster than we were. We needed that advantage. It was all we had."

The captain thought about what he said. "Okay, write it up. I want a complete report of what you did." He nodded at the systems engineer. "And Edmund, thank you. You might be somewhat over the top at times, but you sure saved our butts today."

Edmund smirked. "Yup, I sure did. I knew that device could be used as a weapon. None of us would have made it without that. I'm glad I was there and that I had the expertise to work it. There's no way around it—you needed me, and that's the only reason we're still alive. You would've been toast without me."

The captain held his gaze. "Yes, that's true. But let's dial down the obnoxious side just a bit, okay?"

The systems engineer laughed. "Yes, Captain. But I'm really proud of what I did. I wasn't even sure I could do that. It was just a theory before this, and it was never tested. But I had to try it. It was all we had, and I'm glad it worked."

"Well, it sure did, and it was successful. We owe you."

Edmund grinned. "I'll remember you said that, Captain."

William chuckled. "Yes, I'm sure you will, Edmund."

The navigator looked up. "We'll dock in the spaceship in ten seconds, Captain."

"Excellent. Well done, Marcus."

"Thank you, Captain." Marcus adjusted the controls as the shuttle eased into the spaceship and came to a rest with a soft thud.

William breathed a sigh of relief as they exited the shuttle and returned to the bridge of the ship. It was good to be back.

"I'll start on that report, Captain." Edmund turned and left the bridge.

After the door closed behind Edmund, Marcus shook his head. "Obnoxious doesn't even come close to describing him."

William sighed. "Marcus, he saved our butts down there. We would have been dead without him. Obnoxious? Maybe. Genius? Yes. And we need him." He let out a loud exhale.

"True, Captain." The navigator chuckled. "As soon as we're on our way, I'll write up my report as well."

The relief pilot stood up. "It's good to see you back. Everything's fine up here."

"Thank you, Kurt. I'll take over now," Marcus said as he sat down and looked over the navigation panel. He entered new coordinates, his fingers flying over the controls as he made adjustments. "Okay, Captain, we're out of here and now on our way to our next destination—Outpost 426."

"Take your time, Marcus. We need some rest here."

"So I guess Outpost 391 is a no-go, right?"

William guffawed. "You could say that, Marcus. And I'm sure glad we are still here to say it."

"I wish we had weapons with us down there."

The captain nodded. "Next time we take a security officer with us, even if we don't think it's necessary."

"Good idea, Captain."

"And Marcus?" The captain held the navigator's gaze. "You were right. Those rumors were true." He shook his head. "I saw the bones left behind from one member of the previous crew. Those creatures killed him. I even found a notebook left behind."

Marcus looked up at the captain, his eyes wide. "What?"

The captain nodded. "It's all true. They were killed down there."

"But what happened to the rest of the crew?"

The captain pursed his lips. "I would guess that the creatures killed everyone who was on the surface, and any bones have long since been blown away by the strong winds."

Marcus's face paled. "And their landing shuttle?"

"Well, considering what those creatures were doing to ours, they could easily have torn it apart, and the pieces would have blown away with that wind, too."

"But what about their spacecraft? That would have still been in orbit, right?"

William shook his head. "I don't have an answer for that." A shiver ran up his spine.

Marcus nodded and returned to the navigation panel.

Thinking about how close they had come to not getting out in time, the captain took a deep breath and let it out slowly. "I'll brief both of you on what I found. But first, let's get our reports written up. I'll look them over and send them in. We don't want to be the next rumor that people talk about."

~~~

STRANGE ENCOUNTER

Marcie pulled her long hair back into a ponytail, grabbed her purse, and ran out to her car. She couldn't wait to see Kevin. Being with him was always the high point of her day. She wished the relationship would become even more, and she trusted that would happen someday. For now, she didn't want to push too hard.

Glancing at her watch and seeing that she was running late, she decided to take a shortcut to his house. The road ran along the beach, curving with the shoreline. She rolled down the window and smelled the tangy, salty air from the ocean. A few minutes later, she slowed down as she spotted a barrier across the road with a large sign printed in red letters: ROAD CLOSED.

Why was the road closed? She was already running late and didn't want to go back and take the long way. Maybe it would be okay. She maneuvered her car around the barrier and slowly inched forward, staying alert for any problems. Sand covered the road in patches, but she didn't think it was bad enough to close the entire road. Thinking the worst was over, she kept going.

Ten minutes later, she wondered if this was a mistake. The sand swirled over the road and it was hard to tell where the pavement was. What if she got stuck? She'd never get to Kevin's. Stopping the car, she reached for her cell phone and called him.

He picked up immediately. "Hey, babe."

"Hey," she replied, already smiling. "I'm halfway to your place on the beach road, but the road is closed and covered with sand. I'm getting worried that I'll be stuck here." Would he think she was stupid for taking this road past the warning sign?

He laughed. "You won't believe this," he said. "I did the same thing. I was on my way to meet you and surprise you, and I also took the shortcut. And it's closed on my side too."

Marcie gasped. "It is? Where are you now?"

"Close to you. Stay put. I'll be there in a few minutes. See you soon, babe."

She hung up the phone. No matter what happened, he always made her feel better. But why would the road be closed? A shiver ran up her spine.

A couple minutes later, she saw his silver SUV coming toward her. He waved at her as he stopped his car in front of hers and got out.

Marcie got out of her car and gestured toward him. "Hey, you're in the way. I'm trying to get through," she joked.

Kevin laughed, picked her up, and spun her around before putting her down and planting a big kiss on her lips. "I missed you and I love you," he murmured.

"Mmm, that was nice. I love you too." She gazed into his warm hazel eyes. She could look at him all day. "Hey, doesn't the air here feel different?"

"What do you mean?"

"Like it's thick. Something is weird. It feels uncomfortable." Movement and reflected light caught her attention and she glanced to the side. "What the ..."

Kevin followed her gaze. "Is that ..."

Marcie stared at what looked like an alien spacecraft and two dark gray alien beings studying something on the beach. "That can't be ..."

Kevin's voice was quiet. "Well, that explains why the road is closed in this section."

Marcie's palms were damp as her anxiety increased. "Maybe we should get out of here."

"You're probably right. We don't want to get caught here. And who knows what those aliens would do if they saw us."

"Yeah, let's go. Something feels really eerie. Maybe that's why the air feels thick here. Something's really wrong."

"Yes, something does feel off. I don't like it. We need to get going."

"I agree. I'm hungry anyway."

Kevin nodded. "Me too. I would love a big fat burger." As the words left his mouth, the air in front of him sizzled. He gasped as sparkles formed and it slowly morphed into a hamburger floating in the air in front of him. He hesitated and then grabbed it. Inhaling deeply, he glanced at Marcie. "This smells wonderful. Do you think it's edible?"

Marcie stared at him, her mouth open. "I'm ... not sure. I don't think we should trust it. But I'd really like a burger too." The air sizzled, sparkles formed, and a burger materialized in front of her.

The tantalizing aroma of the beef and spices reached her and she grabbed the burger, which was still warm. "I'm starving and this smells too good. Bizarre or not, I'm eating it."

"Me too," Kevin mumbled around a mouthful of his burger. "This is really good."

They finished their burgers in silence for a few minutes, then Marcie licked her fingers. "Hey, we need napkins now." The air sizzled and sparkles formed, and a small pile of napkins appeared in her hand. She gaped at them for a few moments, and then handed one to Kevin and wiped her mouth with another.

Marcie stared at Kevin. The air around them felt electrified. "What if whatever we ask for appears?"

Kevin gave a nervous laugh. "Then I'd like a thousand dollars." Within a minute, a large pile of money appeared in his hand.

Marcie gasped. "I want a million dollars!" Many large stacks of bills appeared on the ground in front of her, and she started laughing and picking up a few handfuls of bills. "This is impossible. It must be some kind of joke."

Kevin shrugged. "Well, the burger was real. And delicious, too."

Marcie giggled. "All I really want is to be with you."

Kevin leaned forward and kissed her soft lips, then wrapped his arms around her. "You already have that," he murmured in her ear.

He pulled back and gazed into her eyes. After clearing his throat, he spoke slowly. "I want the most beautiful diamond engagement ring." Within moments, a gold ring with a large diamond appeared in his hand.

Marcie's eyes grew wide. "Is that ... for me?"

A shout from the beach startled them, and they turned toward the sound. Two uniformed men were confronting the aliens. One of the aliens pointed at the officers and the men instantly vanished in a cloud of gray smoke which quickly dissipated. The officers were gone, nowhere to be seen.

Kevin pushed Marcie toward her car. "We need to get out of here. Now. Before they see us."

Without another word, they got into their vehicles. Marcie placed the money she had grabbed and the remaining napkins on the seat next to her. After Kevin backed up his car and gave her room, Marcie made a quick U-turn, and they drove down the road toward the barrier.

Marcie struggled to breathe. She could not take a deep breath. The air felt heavy and thick, even oppressive, pressing on her throat. Sizzling sounds permeated the air, and she drove faster, the hair on her neck standing out.

As they approached the barrier that closed the road, the air thinned out and felt more normal again. She took a deep breath and let it out slowly.

After driving a short distance beyond the barrier, Marcie pulled to the side of the road, and Kevin pulled up behind her.

Kevin got out of his car and came to Marcie, and she rolled down the window. He leaned in. "You okay?"

Marcie nodded. "Yes, but ..."

"But what?"

She hesitated. "It was hard to breathe back there. Did you feel that too?"

Kevin nodded, and she continued. "And the money has disappeared. Same with the napkins. What we received at the beach has vanished. It only existed there."

Kevin stared at her for a few moments. "That was the strangest thing I ever experienced."

"Spooky and scary. I hope it doesn't have any lasting effects." She glanced around. "But at least we're out of there. And we're okay."

"I know." He gestured back to where they had been. "Too bad we couldn't have kept what we manifested there."

Marcie gasped. "The ring?"

He shook his head. "Gone." He reached forward and brushed the back of his fingers over her cheek. "But I'll get another one. A real one."

She swallowed. "I'd like that."

"And you know what is real?"

"What?"

"My love for you." He smiled. "And this." He placed a soft kiss on her lips. "Let's go get some lunch. If those burgers weren't real either, we still need some food."

She laughed as her stomach gurgled. "You're right. Sounds good to me."

"And then we can go ring shopping and get one for real. We'll do it right."

She hesitated, then looked into his eyes. "Would you have done that even if it didn't manifest for free back there? Are you ready for that?"

"Marcie, you are the best thing that ever happened to me. I don't know what happened out there, but whatever it was, it made me treasure what we have even more. That might have been strange and bizarre, but what we have is real. And I want to make this permanent."

She smiled and got out of the car, closing the door behind her. "I would like that too."

"Besides," he added, chuckling, "it has a nice ***ring*** to it."

Marcie broke out in a loud laugh and hugged him. "I love you."

"Hey, before they come after us and make us disappear, let's go grab some lunch."

She nodded. "Still want hamburgers?"

"No, maybe pizza would be better now."

"And garlic bread."

The air sizzled around them and a box of pizza materialized on the hood of her car with a bag on top of it. They stared at it unmoving. Her hand shaking, she stepped over and opened the bag. "It's garlic bread," she said softly.

His voice cracked. "What happened to us?"

"I'm not sure. Are we still affected by something alien? Was it the burgers we ingested? Or lingering effects from the air back there? Do we have new abilities? Or is something else going on?" She rubbed the goosebumps appearing on her arms.

"I don't know. I think we need to get away from here."

She shivered. "I feel cold now. I wish I had my jacket." The air shimmered and a jacket materialized over her arm. She gasped, her eyes wide, and she jerked her arm back. The jacket fell to the ground and she stood there staring at it. "What the ..."

After a few minutes, Kevin picked up the jacket. "Maybe it's just a leftover residue from the energy there. It probably won't last."

Her voice shook. "And if it continues?"

He hesitated before speaking. "We will need to be careful with what we wish for. And, whatever it is, we both have it. We'll figure out something."

"I'm spooked, Kevin."

"Me too." He took her in his arms and held her for a few moments and then pulled back. "Let's get out of here—I really don't want to stay here. And let's go get lunch for now and think about this for a while."

"Okay." As she took a step and started to reach for her car door, it opened on its own, waiting for her.

Marcie shrieked and jumped back, staring at the open door.

Kevin squeezed her hand. "Let's get farther away from here and give it some time. I'm sure it will dissipate."

Marcie nodded, not saying another word. After waiting another few minutes without anything else happening, she got in the car. Her hands shaking, she gripped the wheel and murmured, "I want a thousand dollars." Money appeared on the seat next to her. Tears sprang to her eyes as fear flooded her body.

"Please keep me safe," she whispered as the car started on its own and slowly drove forward.

~~~

ALIEN ATTACK

A **loud explosion** boomed and echoed in the city across the river. Cammie pulled her hand back from Brian's grasp as they rushed down the street along the river. She couldn't believe what was happening.

Staring at the artillery raining down on the buildings across the rushing river, Cammie gasped and felt weak. "What the ..." Panic stricken, she stared at her husband. "Mom and Dad are still in the city," she yelled, her voice sounding hoarse and desperate. "We have to get them out."

"Cammie, your parents are trained scientists. They're okay." Brian seemed calm and in control as he grabbed her hand again. "And we need to get out of here. Now." She could hear the urgency in his voice. "Come on. It's not safe to stay here." He pulled her down the street, and she struggled to keep up with his long strides.

Cammie gestured helplessly at the continuing explosions and smoke in the city. "But ... but we are being attacked—by alien vessels." Breathing hard, her voice came out in a rush. "Alien spaceships attacking our city, our people. We need to do something. Someone needs to help us."

Brian looked back at her, a warning in his eyes. "We can't discuss this here. Wait until we're safe."

He rushed down the street and turned into an alley, pulling her along, and stopped in front of an unmarked, dark green door.

Blocking a small gray panel next to the door, he punched in a code and waited, his hand hovering over the doorknob. He glanced around as the door clicked open. Quickly opening the door, he ushered his wife in, hurrying in after her.

Cammie stared at him as fear and confusion rushed through her. "What is going on?" Her eyes searched his for answers. "What do you know about this?"

"Cammie, there's a lot you don't know, and I'm sorry we couldn't tell you." He paused for a few moments, considering what to say, and then continued. "Your parents have one of the most dangerous jobs. They are fighting back against the alien attack. They are protecting us and are highly trained for this. But what they are doing will make them targets themselves and put them in further danger."

Her mouth dry, she took a quick breath, not knowing what to say. How could she not have known any of this? Baffled and confused, she stared at her husband.

Brian remained calm and watched her as he continued. "Your parents have gone through rigorous training for this, and they know what they're doing. They are the best at this job and all that it requires, and they are taking precautions. Trust me."

He moved to a desk and sat down. "Come here. Look at this." He turned on a computer, and his fingers danced over the keyboard. The screen lit up with images of the city and clearly showed the alien weapons raining down.

A quick flash of blue light on the right of the screen got Cammie's attention. "What was that?" She pointed at the monitor.

Brian turned his gaze to her. "That was your parents fighting back." He pulled a chair over for her to sit next to him. "Sit down. Watch." He nodded toward the screen.

"How do you know this?" she whispered. "How are you involved?"

A few more flashes of blue light, and two alien scout ships fell and crashed. Her eyes grew wide as she watched. More flashes of blue and more crashes.

Brian squeezed her hand. "I designed the defense system your parents are using. I've been working with them."

Cammie stared at him, her mouth open. "What?"

He smiled nervously and then sighed. "It's top secret and on a need-to-know basis only. I am not allowed to discuss it. But you have a right to know, especially now."

Cammie's eyes went back to the screen, watching intently. One more weapon dropped, and another flash of blue lit up the screen. Another dark gray metal ship fell and crashed in a cloud of smoke. She stared at the monitor, barely able to breathe.

A few minutes went by, and there was only silence. The attack seemed to have either paused or ended. Gray clouds of dust and debris filled the air, but there was no more artillery fire.

A double flash of orange lit up the screen. Brian frowned and his fingers flew over the keyboard. An encrypted message of numbers appears. Brian pressed more keys, and a written message appeared.

"Warning. One stealth enemy vessel has sneaked through and gotten away. We couldn't get this one. It's now heading your way. Be careful. Get them if you can. Take precautions."

Brian turned to a second computer, wiggled the mouse, and navigated to a concealed application. Hunched over the keyboard, he entered a few codes. The monitor lit up with a view of the darkening sky above them. The black outline of an alien spaceship became visible, flickering in and out of view.

Intensely focused, Brian hit more keys and then hit *Enter*. "I think I got them," he murmured, watching the screen.

A sudden brilliant flash of light flooded the monitor and a loud rumbling noise sounded. Then a huge crash of metal and an explosion shook the ground and rattled the walls.

"Got them." He quickly tapped the keys and sent a message.

Cammie stared at her husband. "You took them down?"

Brian nodded. "Yes. We have to do it this way, with weapons fired remotely and under cover. Any visible weapons we put in the air to target them get taken out by them immediately. But I got them." He ran his fingers through his hair and let out a long breath.

A quick triple flash of blue flickered on the screen, and Brian smiled. "It's over."

Bewildered, Cammie stared at him. After another minute, she glanced at the monitor and then back at her husband. "What do you do? What do my parents do?"

He raised an eyebrow. "As you know, I am an aerospace engineer. But what you don't know is that I have been working with the government under a top-secret agency. Your parents work there too." He watched her, giving her time to absorb the information. "We are keeping you safe. We are keeping everyone safe. Our city. The world."

Cammie felt numb. "And the aliens are gone? All of them? And my parents are okay? You're sure?"

"Yes. The code they flashed indicated they are safe. No more aliens detected."

The monitor beeped, and Brian pressed a few keys. A string of numbers ran across the bottom of the screen. Brian pressed more keys, and the numbers changed into words.

"Last target has been taken down. Good job. Attack is over. All targets annihilated and threat has been removed. We are safe."

Cammie stared at Brian. What else didn't she know? What other secrets were there? She gazed into her husband's warm brown eyes, seeing a combination of intelligence, focus, caring, and love. She felt like she barely knew him and was getting to know him all over again. A rush of admiration and awe ran through her. What more was there to learn about him under that kind, warm, and mysterious outside? She knew she loved him and trusted him with her life, but this took it to a new level.

"I have never lied to you," he said, his gaze holding hers. "This was something I was not allowed to discuss with anyone, and I apologize for keeping you in the dark. I wish I could have shared it sooner, but I could not. But things have changed now, and I will tell you more and fill you in."

Cammie nodded. "Yes, please. I want to know more. I want to know *you*. There seems to be a lot I don't know." She reached for his hand and leaned against him, her head pressing into his chest.

He raised her face to his and pressed his lips to hers. Warmth flooded her as she kissed him back.

He pulled back and chuckled. "We will discuss everything, I promise. For now, let me check in with my superiors. Just sit tight for a few minutes, okay?" He kissed her again and his face lit up with the familiar look of love that Cammie knew so well. "Trust me. I am the same person you always knew. And I love you more than you could possibly know, and I always will." He smiled and then turned back to the computer, his fingers flying over the keyboard.

Bewildered and amazed, Cammie watched him and then sighed as she began to relax. The city and the residents would need a lot of help and there would be a lot of clean-up needed. But for now, her parents were safe and the city was safe. That was a relief. But she could barely comprehend that her husband and her parents were integral in making that happen.

A flood of awe, respect, and admiration moved through her, and she felt her body heat up. Cammie observed her husband working, feeling intrigued by his expertise and knowledge.

Brian turned to her. "I have informed my superior of everything. They are sending agents right now to handle the clean-up and extraction of data, equipment, and any alien beings. We need to stay here for a little bit and not be seen. I need to remain anonymous and not associated with any of this."

"How did you learn all this and know how to fight them?"

Brian shook his head. "This is not the first time they have attacked us, and we have learned a lot each time they invade and assault us. We expected this. We knew they were coming and we were ready." He gestured toward the computers. "And this time, I believe we breached their communications and sent back a message with a coded virus to their leader. It will be a while before they try again. If they ever do."

"I'm overwhelmed and impressed." Goosebumps rose on her arms and she rubbed them. "And I love you. I'm here for you, whatever you need."

He leaned in and kissed her. "I love you. And I always knew I could count on you."

Cammie gazed into her husband's warm brown eyes that she knew so well. What more would she learn? Both horrified at what happened and intrigued by what she was now learning, she looked forward to finding out more.

Brian took her hand and kissed her palm, sending a tingle up her arm. "You are now part of this and cannot talk about any of this to anyone. Understand?"

"Yes," she whispered, admiration and love filling her. She knew nothing would ever be the same again. "And I love you."

~~~

NEW EARTH

B*EEP BEEP BEEP!*

Nikki peered at the navigation panel and adjusted the controls. Then she reviewed the instrument readout—they were now back on course. Every now and then, something altered their course. There were numerous and constant variables and possibilities, and a slight adjustment was periodically needed. She checked it often, and was glad the parameters were set to sound an audible alarm if anything needed attention.

"Everything okay?" Captain Rosita Esperanza Reyes sat behind her on the bridge. She was a good captain—strong, capable, knowledgeable—and always maintaining control. And she was also fair with everyone. Nikki liked, admired, and respected her.

"Yes, just a minor adjustment needed. We're on course." Nikki glanced at the captain and then looked back at the controls. She checked the transmission data and nodded. Everything was good.

She tapped her foot as a wave of anxiety moved through her. It had been eight months since they had left Earth. She clearly remembered the launch, the strong vibration, the intense shaking, and the heavy pull on her body as the ship took off. She remembered closing her eyes and praying, as fear shook her body every bit as powerfully as the thrust engines.

They had left Earth out of desperation. It was their last chance. The violence on Earth had increased to an unsustainable level. Country against country, and person against person. Fighting about land, race, nationality, religion ... and the greed of the wealthy that had plunged so many people below poverty levels. But the violence was the worst part. It had kept escalating. She kept hoping for peace and trusted in the goodness of people, but lasting peace never came. And finally—the last devastating action. The nuclear war. The bombs. She shivered as the graphic memories hit her.

As life on Earth continued to become unlivable, a small group of people were chosen to relocate to another planet that had been discovered a few years back. A habitable planet, much like Earth, a short distance away through a wormhole. Breathable atmosphere, temperature within a tolerable range, and water. It was workable. And it was the only way mankind would survive. They needed to leave Earth and start again.

It had been planned for years, even before the recent wars. It had been a just-in-case, worst-case scenario. But it happened. They would have to completely start over. Life on a new planet.

If only this weren't necessary. But it was. The horrific memories were burned into her brain, and she could never forget them. She shook her head, trying to rid herself of those horrible images of death, pain, and suffering.

After what happened on Earth, they had all decided and agreed to bring no weapons whatsoever. They knew the onboard 3-D printer would be able to create a weapon if needed against an unknown danger on this new planet, but it was unlikely that would be necessary. And after what had escalated on Earth, they wanted nothing to do with weapons.

Now she needed to look to the future. The top scientific minds were onboard, and they had the skills and ability to create a new home. A new life. She needed to stay positive. There was no other choice.

And Jonathan was onboard too. An expert in both aerospace and mechanical engineering, he had been one of the first few chosen for this endeavor. Nikki had met him three months ago as they were busy with preparations for this mission. Their connection was instant and strong, and she was glad he was here. She needed a friend, a partner, and a lover to help in this transition.

They were now almost at the new planet. This had to work. She checked the navigation display again and let out a slow breath. They would be there tomorrow morning.

Eva came by right on time and relieved her on the bridge. Nikki caught her up to date, stretched, and then left. It was good to get away for a little bit. The staff meeting in preparation for landing would be in two hours, and she was feeling antsy.

She went to the small gym at the back of the ship. It would be good to work off her nervous energy, and she knew it was important to stay in shape for whatever was coming. She stepped onto the treadmill, adjusted the speed and grade, and was soon lost in her thoughts as she jogged.

Two hours later, after a shower and a quick meal, she sat at the conference table in the meeting room. Captain Reyes commanded the room, her powerful presence projecting strength and instilling confidence in all the staff. "Okay everyone, we will be landing tomorrow morning on schedule. Jamil," she said, turning to the geologic and atmospheric expert. "How are conditions on our new planet?"

Jamil looked up from his notes. "Fine, Captain. From what we can tell, the air is breathable, a combination of oxygen and nitrogen, and temperature in a comfortable range. Humidity is low but reasonable. I'll know more after we land and will check it again before we leave the ship. But it all looks good by my calculations."

"Thank you, Jamil." She turned to Haruto Tominaga, renowned for his expertise in physics and also for being a top-notch musician. "Haruto, what is your analysis of our approach, landing, and anything you can foresee for the next few days?"

Haruto cleared his throat. "Everything is good, Captain. I foresee no problems at this point. My calculations show that as we enter the atmosphere ..." As he went into further detail, Nikki's mind wandered to the last time she had heard him play the cello. He was magnificent when he played, and the music always deeply moved her. She hoped he had brought the cello onboard. She closed her eyes, hearing the melodies in her mind.

She suddenly opened her eyes and saw Jonathan watching her, a smirk on his face. She smiled at him and looked around at the rest of the crew. The level of expertise and experience in the room was astounding, and the diversity in background filled her with hope for a compassionate human experience in building a new world. These people were committed to making a good start for all of humanity. She focused again on the captain.

"... So you all know what to do when we land," the captain was saying. "I want the first crew of twelve to scout out the area for thirty minutes only. Take measurements, be aware of your surroundings, and observe everything carefully. Then we meet at the entrance to the ship. If there are no problems, and everything looks good, the second crew of twelve will join the first crew, and we will explore farther out. I want feedback as to possible locations for housing and for planting. Look for a source of water. I want to know all impressions and everything that you observe, including any possible problems. Then we will systematically expand our search area from there." She looked at each member. "And the first team, for the initial outing, do not go more than three hundred yards. I want our first excursion safe and close. Understood?"

***

At dinner, Nikki barely touched her food. "Eat something," Jonathan told her, as he took another bite of chicken marsala. "You need to eat." He gestured at her food with his fork. "You need your strength."

Nikki stared at her food and pushed it around, and finally speared a potato with her fork. "I know. I'm just too nervous to eat. But you're right." She shoved the potato into her mouth. "Mmmm, this is actually really good. You're right. I need to eat."

"I'm really excited and also a little nervous." Jonathan reached over and squeezed her hand, his rich dark skin in contrast to her pale, freckled skin. "There will be so much to do here. And so many possibilities for this new world." He took another bite of chicken.

"I know. This world holds so much promise. And we have really good people onboard."

"Only the best," he said as he chewed. "Including you," he added, smiling.

They finished eating, listening to the excited chatter fill the small cafeteria as other crew members sat down with their meals. Nikki and Jonathan got up, cleaned their table, and placed the dirty dishes in the pile to be washed.

Jonathan pulled Nikki into his arms and kissed the top of her head. "We're landing tomorrow," he said softly. "It's amazing we're actually here."

"I know. I can't believe it's here already. I'm not sure I'll be able to sleep tonight." She buried her face in his chest, feeling his warmth. She treasured the few moments of peace and comfort with him before the commotion and tasks she knew would be coming the next day.

Once back in her quarters, Nikki read through all the information she had on this new planet for the hundredth time. She had read it through so many times that she had it almost memorized, but she needed to read it again anyway. This was going to be their new home.

As expected, she barely slept. She kept waking up throughout the night, checking the clock, and trying to go back to sleep. She finally slept a couple hours and then bolted awake at 6:00 a.m., covered in sweat.

After a quick shower, she nervously picked at and managed to eat a breakfast of oatmeal, blueberries, and a hard-boiled egg, washed it down with orange juice, and then hurried back to the bridge. It was almost time to land on New Earth.

"No problems," Eva said and smiled when Nikki approached to relieve her. "We're on course, and everything looks fine." Eva yawned and quickly left the bridge, as Nikki thanked her.

Nikki sat at the navigation board and checked the time, course, coordinates, trajectory, speed, and other readouts. All looked good. They would touch down in one hour.

It was hard to sit still. They were finally reaching the end of this part of their journey and starting a whole new one, full of unknowns. A bright new beginning. This had to work, and she was sure it would. This was not going to be the end of humanity.

She stared at the planet as it came into view and grew larger on the monitor. Her heart fluttered. It was beautiful. Blues, greens, and browns, plus white clouds. It already looked like home. She licked her dry lips. They were almost there. Almost home.

Alarm klaxons blared throughout the ship. "Please prepare for landing," the automated voice announced. It was time.

Creases appeared on her forehead as she focused and concentrated, guiding the ship down to the planet's surface. She reduced the speed and changed the angle. She felt the pressure on the ship change. Almost down. A loud whine filled the bridge, followed by a whooshing noise. The ship thumped and then lightly bounced as it landed on the surface, thumped once more, and then came to a rest. Silence.

Nikki glanced at Captain Reyes and then looked out the main viewport. A small brownish dust cloud had been kicked up and it momentarily blocked her view. The dust cloud slowly dissipated, and as the view cleared, she looked out in wonder.

A panorama opened before her—brown dirt, a few small green plants, and a structure off to the left side. Brilliant sunlight flooded the entire vista. It looked sparse, but beautiful. The first view of their new home.

Captain Reyes leaned forward. "Nikki, call the first landing crew to meet in fifteen minutes in Landing Bay One."

"Yes, Captain." She transmitted the message to the crew and immediately received confirmation from each one. "They're all ready, Captain."

Fifteen minutes later, the twelve crew members stood in Landing Bay One. "Everyone ready?" Captain Reyes looked at each member. "Jamil, any update on atmospheric conditions? Are we good to go?"

"Yes, Captain," Jamil answered. "Everything is as expected. It is breathable and within an acceptable range. I see no problems."

"Good. When we descend onto the planet," she continued, addressing the entire group, "be careful with everything, from walking to breathing. No matter how prepared we are, it will be somewhat different in real time and physically being on a new world. I will remain on the planet with you but at the entrance to the ship in case of any problems. And don't forget—for our initial outing, go out no more than three hundred yards, and we meet back here in thirty minutes. Are we all clear?" Everyone nodded. "Good. Then let's go."

It was time. Jonathan punched the buttons and the door slowly opened with a soft whoosh. A breezy warmth with a light but foreign fragrance reached them as the first twelve slowly descended the six stairs and took their first steps on the new planet.

It was magnificent. Nikki took a deep breath. It was dusty, but sweet. Clean. Breathable. Warm.

Jonathan moved next to her and rubbed her back. "You doing okay?"

She nodded. "Our first steps on a new planet. This is beyond exciting."

"I know. This will be our new home."

Nikki pointed to the left. "Let's check out that structure. I want to see what that is."

She felt her excitement building. What wonders awaited them on this new world?

Nikki felt Jonathan's warm hand clasp hers, and they walked together toward the structure. What was it? Was it a fort? A home? A shelter? Who or what had built this? Had there been other beings here before them?

Reaching the structure, she realized it was larger than it had initially appeared. There were three smaller structures attached to the first, with large rooms inside. They hesitantly entered the first part of the building.

A tremble of fear coursed through Nikki, and goosebumps rose on her arms. She looked around in the first structure, exploring. There were three rooms and steps that led up to a second level. It had obviously been built by an intelligent species. How was that possible? This planet had no known life forms other than plants.

Something caught her eye. Something dark on the ground near one wall. *What was that?* She stepped closer.

Her hand started reaching toward it. Then she quickly pulled it back and gasped.

NO!

She held her breath. She couldn't breathe. Her hand flew to her mouth, her eyes wide with shock.

Jonathan was at her side and she pointed. She heard his sharp intake of breath.

A gun lay on the ground. A man-made handgun from Earth. A human weapon.

Humans had been here before and they had brought weapons with them. Where were the humans now? What happened to them? Had they defended themselves against aliens? Had they killed each other on this planet? Was this going to be no different than how it was on Earth?

161

Excited but muffled shouts from other crew members sounded a short distance away.

Nikki looked into Jonathan's eyes. "What happened here? What happened to these people? And how can we tell our crew? Humans have been here before."

Jonathan swallowed hard. "We need to tell Captain Reyes. She needs to know this."

Nikki nodded, feeling the lump in her throat. "Will we ever learn to live in peace?"

His jaw clenched. "I don't know," he whispered. "After all this time and all we have been through, I have to believe humans have evolved enough that we are beyond this."

She stared at the gun and then looked away. "I sure hope so."

Jonathan let out a long breath. "I guess we'll find out," he murmured.

"Well, we've come a long way. Let's trust that we have grown enough and will no longer resort to this," Nikki said softly, reaching for his hand.

"Yes. And that we continue to grow and evolve. Let's hope for much better days for all of us and for all of humanity." His warm hand clasped hers tightly as they turned and slowly left the structure to rejoin their crew.

~~~

DIMENSIONS OF TRAVEL

I **looked into** Michael's warm, brown eyes. I loved him and trusted him. But this was crazy. What he was saying couldn't be real.

My heart pounded as Michael grabbed my hand. "Come with me, Sara. I'll show you. I'll prove it. You can be a witness."

I stared at him and smirked. "You can't be serious." I rolled my eyes. "A parallel universe. No way."

"Sara, I promise. It's real. And it's safe."

"This is insane." I crossed my arms defiantly. "So where is this portal? How do we get there?" I tapped my foot. Michael was a gifted research scientist and had a great imagination, but this was ludicrous.

He calmly looked into my eyes and squeezed my hand. "There's a portal at the beach. It works." He licked his lips. "I swear. Just let me show you."

I shook my head and sighed. What did I have to lose? "Fine," I stated, deciding to humor him. "Show me."

His face lit up. "Trust me, Sara." He leaned in and kissed me lightly on the lips. He smiled and his eyes sparkled.

He set my soul on fire, and I would do anything for him. He was the most exciting and amazing man I had ever met. But this was still absurd. I hoped he wasn't losing his grasp of reality. But I had to believe him. "Okay. Take me."

Twenty minutes later, we got out of the car at the beach. "There," he said pointing. "Come with me. The portal opens at set times. The next one is in five minutes."

I took a deep breath of the salty, tangy, ocean air, feeling it fill my lungs. Slowly releasing my breath, I looked out over the sparkling white sand, seeing nothing out of the ordinary. An empty beach with the ocean lapping up onto the shore, the whoosh of the waves intoxicating.

I did trust Michael. But this was beyond my limit of what I could comprehend and believe. I turned to him. "So this will take us to an alternate universe?"

He smiled. "Yes. We've done extensive research. It's real. It's simply shifting into a new dimension along distinct energy specifications."

I swallowed hard, my body trembling. "Is it dangerous?"

"No." He hesitated. "Not that we know of, anyway." He laughed and took my hand, the warmth of his strong hand enveloping mine. "I've never shown this to anyone else." His voice was soft, filled with wonder and a touch of nerves. "Are you ready?"

"Michael, I don't see anything here. This is—"

"You can trust me. I will never hurt you, Sara."

We walked across the soft, white sand, our feet sinking in with each step. He led me to a patch of sand that was slightly darker and set in a small depression.

It seemed ridiculous. "Are you sure this—"

"Shhh. Close your eyes." His voice was both calm and commanding.

As I closed my eyes, I briefly saw him remove a small device from a pocket. After hearing a few clicks, a buzzing sound surrounded me, and the air felt electrified. Fear crept up my spine and my teeth started chattering. I wanted to open my eyes, but a combination of fear and a strange pressure kept them shut.

Everything slowly eased up and the pressure dissipated. I slowly opened my eyes.

Dizziness rushed over me and I felt confused. Beginning to lose my balance, I started to fall to the side, and I felt Michael's strong hands grab me and hold me to him.

"You okay?" His voice was warm and caring and felt soothing.

I nodded and looked around. We were still on the beach, but everything was different. Instead of an empty beach, there were a few small stands where snacks, jewelry, clothes, and trinkets were being sold. About thirty people milled around on the warm sand.

It looked peaceful, but somehow strange. How could things change so much on the same beach? "Where are we?" My voice was barely audible.

He chuckled. "I'm not sure, to be honest. I believe we're in the same spot in an alternate universe. A parallel universe."

I looked into his eyes. "So this is all happening at the same time as our universe?"

"Yes." He sounded excited. "There are many alternate and parallel universes, times, and spaces, all happening at once. An infinite number."

"But ... that makes no sense. Are you sure this is safe?"

"I think so. I've done it many times already." He pointed down the beach. "Come, let's get something to eat and then go back. I just wanted you to see and experience this."

"But how is this possible?"

Michael laughed. "You mean the physics and logistics of it?" He shrugged. "It's tuning in to a different, specific energy frequency. It's so exciting, but there is so much that we don't understand yet. We are just starting to explore this, and there is still so much to learn."

We started scuffing through the soft sand, and he continued. "But we have determined that there are infinite alternate or parallel universes, all existing at the same time, and we can access them. Each one has its own energy frequency. And most of them have the same people who have made different choices in their lives, and they live out a different life in each one. But some societies developed differently as well."

My forehead scrunched. "So we could meet ourselves here?"

He shrugged. "Possibly. If we are alive in this one and if we came to this beach at this time."

I shuddered. "That's a lot to think about." Even though the scene was serene, it was too much to take in and make sense of, and my nerves felt on edge.

He squeezed my hand and his eyes searched my face. "You doing okay?"

I nodded, feeling confused and overwhelmed.

He led me down the beach to a vendor selling ice cream. "Want one?"

I smiled. I was always up for ice cream.

Michael pointed at the picture of chocolate popsicles. "Two, please," he said to the man standing behind the cart.

The man smiled and handed Michael two wrapped popsicles. Michael paid the vendor, and I unwrapped my ice cream. Biting into the sweet treat, I let the chocolate creaminess swirl around in my mouth. It felt normal and reassuring, and I started feeling better.

"We need to get back," I murmured, taking another bite of ice cream. "I don't want to get stuck here."

"We'll be fine." Michael checked his watch. "Ten more minutes, and the portal will open again." He pointed to another vendor. "Let me buy you something to remember this by, and as proof that we were here."

I hesitated, then sighed. "Okay."

We walked to another vendor who had various pieces of jewelry and other trinkets for sale. A gold pocket watch on a chain got my eye. It brought back memories of my grandfather. He had one just like that. In fact, I remembered he told me he had gotten it on his first wedding anniversary with my grandmother. I still remember the inscription that was inside. *A marriage made in heaven. William & June.* The memory made me smile and I picked up the watch and held it, feeling the coolness of the metal.

Michael paid the vendor, and I started opening the watch to see if there was an inscription in this one, but Michael grabbed my hand. "Come," he urged. "The portal will only be open for a few more minutes. I don't want to miss it."

I quickly closed the pocket watch and we hurried back across the beach. As we scurried across the soft sand, movement got my eye. Turning toward it, I saw a tall, lumbering, hairy creature. Taking in a quick breath, I pointed. "Is that—"

Michael laughed. "Oh, that's right. Bigfoot is in this one, a natural and accepted part of society."

"What?" I watched a few more seconds until Michael pulled me along.

"We don't want to miss the portal opening," he reminded me.

We stood on the same patch of darkened sand, and Michael brought out his device and punched a few buttons. I closed my eyes as the buzzing noise started. The pressure around us increased and the air felt electrified.

As the pressure eased a couple minutes later, I took an unsteady step forward and looked around. An empty stretch of soft, white sand stretched before us. Our beach. No vendors, no people, no Bigfoot. We were home.

Feeling relieved, I let out a long breath. The whole experience was strange. Had we really been in some alternate or parallel universe? What was that place? Was it real? Was it simply some type of hallucination? It made no sense.

Something dropped from my hand, and I didn't even realize I had been holding something. Quickly looking down, I saw the gold pocket watch in the white sand. My hand shaking, I bent down and picked up the watch. It was real. We actually had been somewhere and I brought this back. It again reminded me of my grandfather's watch ... I opened it up and saw there was an inscription inside, and I eagerly read it.

I gasped and read it again.

A marriage made in heaven. William & June.

That was impossible. How could ...

I turned toward Michael. "How ... how ..."

He smiled. "I have so much more to show you. This is just the start."

~~~

HIDDEN THREAT

K yle shrieked and scooted back in his chair. Goosebumps covered his arms. "I found it."

Richard glanced up from his computer. "You found what?"

"The alien spaceship. It's really there." Kyle scooted forward again and leaned in, peering intently at the monitor. "I knew it was there, but it's been deliberately and carefully hidden. I finally found it." He ran his fingers through his hair. "It is hovering at a height of roughly 20,000 feet, concealed within a gray cloud that never dissipates, and it is over the lake."

Richard got up and walked to Kyle's desk. He leaned over Kyle's shoulder, looking at his computer. "Show me."

"Here." Kyle pointed at a hazy gray blob within a dark gray cloud. "It's hard to see, but the way light is reflected off it shows the shape." He leaned forward, squinting at the screen. "That's it. I knew it was there."

"Are you sure?"

"I'm positive. This is huge progress."

"And the lightning?"

Kyle leaned back in his chair. "I believe the lightning is being generated by the spaceship within the cloud. It is intentional and it is directly hitting that floating barge in the lake."

Richard stared at the screen and then looked at Kyle. "I've been investigating and tracking that barge, but it still doesn't make sense. We can't get inside the barge or even get close enough to really scrutinize it and figure out what it is. And what does the lightning have to do with it? What do you think is going on?"

"Hear me out." Kyle let out a slow breath as he organized his thoughts. "The floating barge we discovered is an alien energy power grid, hidden in plain sight, where people would ignore it. From what you have determined with your analysis, it is virtually indestructible, and yet it contains immense power that the alien ship can utilize and focus for their needs."

"Well, part of that is true. We have not been able to get close enough to investigate it properly. Something keeps us at a distance—almost like a force field that we can't get through. And it does seem to contain a great deal of energy. But it seems to be deliberately trying to stay unobtrusive and be inaccessible. So far, it seems to be impenetrable. We can't even tell what it is constructed from." Richard shook his head. "And we certainly don't know what it's used for—the barge or the energy inside it. Beyond that, what you say is conjecture on your part. We really don't know."

Kyle tilted his head and raised his eyebrows. "Hasn't the lightning seemed strange to you?"

"In what way?"

Kyle thought for a moment before responding. "The lightning seems to be only over the lake in the vicinity of that barge. And it strikes every three days at roughly 1:00 in the afternoon. No storm would be that regular. It never moves inland the way a storm would. There's no rain or wind with it. And it seems to always hit the barge." He gestured toward the screen. "I think it is actually *aimed* at the barge. It is targeting that monstrosity. And when it hits the barge, something happens. You've tested it. What have you found?"

Richard thought back over what he had recently analyzed and evaluated over the past month since being assigned to this investigation, and when he spoke, his voice grew more excited. "Something inside the barge lights up. Something gets activated in there, and there is an increase in temperature and energy. But so far, there's nothing we can understand or figure out. We don't really know what is happening."

"Exactly." Kyle leaned forward and his gaze was intense. "I think the lightning is generated by the spaceship that is hovering above it, hidden in that one cloud that never moves or changes."

Richard was silent for a few minutes and then stared at Kyle. "And for what purpose? What do you think is going on?"

Kyle pursed his lips before answering. "I believe they are using that barge as an alien energy grid. It holds and transforms energy. And the lightning is used to activate something within that barge that generates and secures that energy for them, so they have an unending supply."

Richard stared at him. "But we have no proof or evidence of anything. This is all conjecture." He shook his head and looked at his friend. "And for them to use for what?"

Kyle's voice dropped. "My guess is to either attack humans, take over the planet, or annihilate us. Or all of the above." He looked at Richard. "Whatever it is, it's not good. It is definitely an alien presence, they are not friendly, and they must be stopped. Or do you have another theory of what they are doing?"

Richard stared at the monitor. "I do agree it's been strange observing the lightning just in that one spot, hitting the barge every time. It doesn't make sense. And then the barge lights up from inside in such an eerie way, and there's a noticeable buildup of energy. And nothing we do lets us access it or approach it close enough." He shook his head. "But now that you discovered a spaceship above it ... well ... that changes everything."

"Yes, it sure does." Kyle got up and started pacing. "It gives a reason to what is happening. And it's a terrifying reason."

"What you say makes sense. It feels ominous. Another thing I've noticed is that the lightning strikes have been getting closer together. Remember when they were a week apart? Then five days apart? Now it's only three days. And now that we know there is alien intelligence behind it, well, that's a whole new ballgame. We need to inform our supervisor. We need to tell—"

"No. We can't tell anyone. I know they sent us here to investigate this. But what I found sounds bizarre. And if they don't believe me and they discredit my evaluation, or if they say no, then our hands are tied." He chewed on his cheek and then sat forward. "I'm afraid of what could happen if we don't take action. And it would need to be soon. I think we have to take care of this ourselves."

Richard spoke softly. "But how?"

"I'm not sure yet. But we need to somehow stop them."

"I still think our boss needs to know. He might have additional information on this. Maybe he knows something and could help us."

Kyle shook his head. "No. Remember the last time we asked him about possible alien spacecraft visiting here? He laughed us out of his office. I don't trust his judgment."

Richard looked around the cramped basement filled with computers and equipment. Finally, he nodded. "Yeah, you might be right. Okay, I'm on board. So how can we stop them? What can we do?"

A small grin lit up Kyle's face. "We can set up a device that will do two things. One, when lightning hits it, it will reflect and transmit an energy pulse back to the source—the alien ship—which would burn out their electronics, computers, and devices. It will basically destroy their ship and possibly blow it up as well." His voice grew more animated and he stopped pacing. "And two, the lightning strike will also set off an explosion on the barge itself and blow up the barge including their energy grid."

Richard shook his head. "I'm not sure about this. I know we can set up an electromagnetic pulse singularity that can do most of that. I'm not sure about destroying the barge, but it would at least do some damage." He thought for a few moments. "But what if the explosion of their energy grid triggers something huge that we can't control? Something worse? Something that can potentially harm or destroy life on Earth?"

"Hey, if we do nothing, we're all dead anyway. We'll either be victims to those alien creatures, or they'll kill us. I'd rather deal with a possible energy shock wave than be taken over or killed by an alien species. So for me, there's no question. It needs to be destroyed, right?"

Richard nodded. "Yes, that does make sense. I agree."

"So we really have no choice. We gotta do this. You with me?"

Richard nodded again. "Okay, I agree. I'm in. So setting up an electromagnetic pulse transmitter is no problem." He thought for a minute and then continued. "And I can get that device set up on the barge. I think I figured out a way to get it placed directly on the barge, even without us getting physically close to it." He drummed his fingers on the table. "I can then have it triggered by the lightning strike to send a pulse back up to the source—to that alien ship." His face grew serious as he continued. "And I can set a slight delay and then an explosion that should take out the barge. Give me a few days to get this all ready."

Kyle smiled and sat down again. "You got it. And we have to time it right to get it set up between lightning strikes, especially since those strikes are getting closer together. We need to know when it's safe to set it up and when it will be triggered. And we're running out of time."

***

Three days later, Richard leaned over Kyle's desk. "It's ready."

Kyle looked up into Richard's excited face. "The electromagnetic pulse device? It's ready?"

Richard nodded. "Yes, the EMP device is all set to go. When was the last lightning strike? It was yesterday, right?"

Kyle glanced at his computer and clicked a few keys. "Yes, it was yesterday, Tuesday. The lightning strikes are now every two days. You have until tomorrow morning to get it in place and programmed, and then there will be another lightning strike tomorrow afternoon, Thursday, at 1:00. That's assuming the lightning pattern doesn't increase to every day."

"Good. This will be ready tomorrow morning. I'll get it all set up."

***

Dark clouds filled the sky on Thursday morning. Kyle turned to Richard. "Will bad weather mess up the EMP device? It is dreary and overcast today. It might even rain."

Richard shook his head. "No, it should be good. As long as our real weather itself doesn't create a lightning strike that would set it off, rather than one from the spaceship. We don't want to send a pulse back to just a rain cloud, and we certainly don't want to alert them and have to do this again. I'm not sure they would let us have another chance. We can't let them know we've detected them. We may only get one shot at this."

Kyle checked the computer for the weather. "It says cloudy all day, chance of light rain, but no thunderstorms in the forecast. That's good."

Richard stood up, took a few steps, and looked around the dark basement. Then he returned to his computer and remotely inspected his equipment one more time. "This had better work."

"It will. You do good work. Relax."

Richard shook his head. "So much can go wrong. And this is too important to mess it up." He started pacing. "I have gone over every setting multiple times. I'm sure it's right. I'm just … I don't know … I want this over."

"Hey, sit down. Do something else for a while. It's only 11:00—we have about two hours before the show begins."

"This had better work."

"Relax. It will. I know you. I know the work you do." Kyle scanned the basement. "Hey, are we safe here if there is a shock wave from the barge explosion?"

Richard nodded. "Yes, we should be good. We're underground, and there's a protective layer built into the ceiling above us that should protect us against heat, radiation, electromagnetic pulses … we should be good."

"How much delay will there be from the pulse going back up to the spaceship before the barge explosion?"

"Fifteen seconds. I hope that will give us enough time to see the results from each event separately and be able to track everything and record data without giving them time to do anything in case they are still able to."

Kyle nodded. "I'm sure it will be fine."

"Hey, did you check the spaceship? Is it still there?"

Kyle glanced at the screen. "Yes, they are there. They are still hiding inside that cloud, but I can detect them. They haven't moved."

"Good." Richard sighed and drummed his fingers on the table. "I hate waiting."

"Hey, let's have an early lunch. Otherwise, you'll drive yourself nuts."

"I know. I've double-checked all the figures. I just … You're right. Let's have an early lunch."

After finishing his sandwich thirty minutes later, Kyle stood up and stretched, then went to his computer and clicked a few keys. "So far, so good," he called back to Richard who was cleaning up the table where they had eaten. "No lightning strike yet, and that spaceship is still in the cloud."

"Good," Richard answered as he went to his computer.

Kyle checked his watch. "We have maybe one hour or less left before—"

A loud sizzling sound came from his monitor, interrupting him. Kyle frantically clicked on a few more keys. "Hey, there was a lightning strike. It came early today. I think—"

A bright light flashed on his screen, and the two men watched the cloud light up where the spaceship had been hiding.

"Wait," Richard said, pointing to the screen. "Was the spaceship hit by the pulse? Why wasn't there a bigger explosion? That ship should have exploded. That should have been huge. Or maybe it just took out their electronics but not the ship? Something's wrong. I don't trust this."

"I know. Something's not right." Kyle clicked on the keys.

A rumble came from the speakers, and the ground shook. Kyle looked up. "That might be the explosion on the barge." The structure of the house above them creaked. "And that could be the shock wave, but it doesn't sound as powerful as it should be."

Richard nodded. "Is the barge destroyed? I have a very uneasy feeling about this. Nothing is going the way we expected. What is happening out there?"

Kyle zoomed in on the image. "Something's wrong. The barge seems damaged, but not destroyed. It has set off some type of energy surge, but ... wait ..."

"What is it?" Richard leaned in closer to the monitor and then returned to his own computer and punched in keys.

Kyle gasped. ***"NOOOO!"***

Richard rushed over. "What? What? Talk to me!"

Sweat beaded up on Kyle's scalp and ran down his neck. "The spaceship that was in the cloud ... it was ... it was a decoy. It wasn't real. It was a shadow meant to draw our attention and fool us. It was a distraction."

177

"What are you talking about?"

"It was a trick—it wasn't a real spaceship. There's another spaceship behind it. A real one ... and it has now been alerted. They know we're aware of them."

Richard stared at him. "What do you mean? Are you sure?"

"Look," Kyle answered, pointing at the screen. "They fooled us. See the shadow here? What I thought was a spaceship?" He saw Richard nod, and he continued. "It's a hologram."

"What? So our EMP didn't reach the spaceship?"

"No, not the real one. There's another one behind that one. I couldn't see it, and I thought we had the authentic real ship."

"So the actual spaceship is untouched?" His eyes widened. "And now they know ..."

"Yes. And another lightning strike from the real one will have dire consequences. Especially now that they know we found them. This will propel them to act sooner to protect themselves. And it will most likely accelerate their agenda for whatever they want to do on our world." His eyes grew large and he swallowed hard past the lump in his throat. "This could mean the end of the world as we know it."

"You can't mean ..."

CRACK!

A flash of lightning lit up the screen. The lightning directly hit the barge, and a blinding light blazed on the monitor.

Kyle and Richard raised their arms to protect their eyes against the brightness as a powerful wave of energy raced toward them a fraction of a second later, obliterating everything in its path.

Kyle barely had time to gasp in shock as his throat burned and closed, cutting off his air supply. His arms flailed and his hair sizzled, as he collapsed on the floor next to Richard's bloated body.

The wave of energy continued to rush onward, decimating everything as it raced forward.

~~~

WINDOW TO THE FUTURE

A liya brushed the hair out of her face as she walked up the grassy incline. For months now, she had wanted to climb to the top of the hill in her neighborhood and see the view. Her breathing heavy and ragged from exertion, she was finally there. A shiver of anticipation ran through her as she neared the crest.

Looking up, her eyes opened wide and she stared at the view at the top of the hill. A ruin was there—part of one, anyway. Just the window was left from some unknown structure. It looked ancient and powerful and she felt drawn to it.

Although exhausted from her hike, and still breathing heavily, she moved toward it, her arms outstretched. Something about it felt awe inspiring and even personal. She needed to be closer to it.

The overwhelming power of the window washed over her as she got near enough to touch it. Tentatively, she reached a trembling hand to the stone. It felt warm and rough, and she placed her hand flat on the rock. Closing her eyes, she took a deep breath.

When she opened her eyes, the view through the ancient window had shifted. Her brow furrowed as she tried to comprehend what she was seeing. Through the window was a barren wasteland. The ground was parched and devoid of life. There were no trees, plants, birds, animals, or people. Just empty, scorched dirt—as though a huge fire or a war or nuclear devastation had blown through the area.

"What am I seeing?" she whispered to the window.

A voice in her head answered. *You are seeing the future of Earth. Years from now, war and greed will have destroyed all life on the planet. However, this can be prevented. It is not too late. The one who can see this is the one who can change it and save the planet. We have been waiting a long time for you to arrive.*

Aliya looked around but saw no one. She looked back at the window. "Who are you?"

We are the gatekeepers of the world. We have been trying to save your planet, but we cannot do it alone.

"But ... but I don't know what to do. How can I save Earth?"

There is a piece missing in the wall surrounding the window. A vital piece that has come loose and fallen out. The missing piece that will save the planet.

"What piece? Where is it? How do I find it?"

It is a crystal that is vital to mankind. In fact, it is vital to all life on Earth. You must find it, plug it back into the wall, and close the loophole that has developed. That loophole created the wars, the greed, the hatred, the fighting, the emptiness, and the catastrophes that have befallen the planet.

"But how do I find this crystal?"

You will know where to look. It is in your possession. It needs to be placed in the wall before the window closes completely and disappears—then it will be too late.

"What kind of crystal?"

You will know it when you see it. You know where it is. Hurry. We are running out of time.

Aliya removed her hand from the wall and took a step back. Was she imagining everything she heard? How would she know what crystal or where it was?

She glanced at the window and the view was back to the way it was before. She could see the blue sky, a few clouds, and the other side of the hill. Her eyes followed a dirt path leading down the hill to a long stretch of beach which lined a huge dark blue ocean. It was hard to tear her eyes away from the view.

After a few minutes, she slowly turned and ran back the way she had come, going back down the hill and along the street to her home. An urgency gnawed at her, and she felt that the voice in her head was real. She had to help. But how?

Once she reached home, something pulled her to the closet in her bedroom. She wasn't sure why, but she opened the closet door and immediately picked up a small wooden box from the floor. Treasures she had been given by her grandfather when he was still alive. She smiled, remembering the smell of sawdust and tools on him, and the jangling of keys that always hung from his belt.

Sitting on the side of her bed, she slowly opened the box. Folded papers, a marble, and a few coins greeted her eyes. And there on the side—what was that? A pink stone—rose quartz. A crystal of love. She didn't remember seeing it there before. Did she simply forget about it?

The crystal began vibrating and emitting a low hum. She instantly knew. Deep inside, without a doubt—this was it. This was the missing piece that was needed.

She picked up the smooth, pink crystal and held it in her hand. It was cool to the touch, but it warmed up as it sat in her hand. She felt the vibration move through her. Goosebumps rose all over her body. She knew what she had to do.

She ran outside, down the street, through the field, and back to the grassy hill. She climbed up to where she was before. The stone window was there. A tremor of doubt ran through her mind, but she felt an urgency within her. She knew this needed to be done as soon as possible.

She approached the window and held up the rose quartz. "Is this it? Is this what was missing?"

Yes. That is the missing piece. The energies of love and compassion have been lost from humanity as mankind turned its back on this force. But this energy is vital for the survival of all life. Without it, the world and all life forms will perish. Time is running out.

"Where do I put this?"

Look for it. You will find it. You will know.

Aliya pulled her hair back and stepped closer to the window. She ran her hands over the rough stones. On the inside ledge on the left side, a gaping hole stared back at her. A deep black emptiness emanated from it. That must be it.

Trembling, she reached forward, her fingers shaking as they held the crystal. She inched it closer. A sudden flash of white light arced from the crystal into the black hole, and the rose quartz slid into place with a soft click.

"Is that what I was supposed to—"

The window vibrated, and she felt the rumbling through the ground under her feet. Bright light flashed through the window and her hand came up to shield her eyes.

After a few moments, a sense of peace settled around her and she opened her eyes and looked through the window. A vast field of pink and yellow flowers greeted her. A rabbit ran through, twitched its nose, and then hopped away. Tall trees shimmered in the distance, their lacy leaves dancing in a light breeze. Two birds sang as they flew past in the sky.

Aliya blinked. The window shimmered and shifted back to the original view. Blue sky, a few clouds, and the grassy hill on the other side.

She stared at the view for a few minutes. "Am I done?"

Yes. You were the only one who could do this. And time was closing fast. We thank you.

"But who are you? Can I see you?"

You will see us soon enough.

A flash of light burst through the window. The stones shimmered for a few moments, and then collapsed into a heap. The window was gone. A small pile of old rocks sat in the grass where the window had been just moments before.

She stood there for a few more minutes.

"Are you still here?"

The only answer was the whisper of a breeze as it rustled the weeds at the top of the hill.

She turned and slowly made her way back down the hill and through the field toward her house.

As she approached the door to her home, the wind picked up, and the breeze turned into a whisper.

We are always here.

~~~

AFTERWORD

Thank you for reading this science fiction short story collection, ***Beyond the Abyss.***

I sincerely hope you enjoyed these stories and that they opened new worlds, sparked your imagination, and sent tingles up your spine as you explored the incredibly exciting world of science fiction!

If you enjoyed these stories, please check out my other short story collections:

- ***Beyond the Abyss*** – Science Fiction
- ***Beyond Terror*** – Thrillers, Horror, and Suspense
- ***Beyond Love*** – Love and Romance
- ***Beyond Connections*** – Family and Relationships

Thank you again for reading ***Beyond the Abyss!***

— *Lynn Miclea*
Author

ABOUT THE AUTHOR

LYNN MICLEA is a writer, author, editor, musician, Reiki master practitioner, and dog lover.

After retiring, Lynn further pursued her passion for writing, and she is now a successful author with many books published and more on the way.

She has written numerous short stories and published many books including thrillers, science fiction, paranormal, romance, mystery, memoirs, a grammar guide, self-help guided imagery, short story collections, and children's stories (fun animal stories about kindness, believing in yourself, and helping others).

She hopes that through her writing she can help empower others, stimulate people's imagination, and open new worlds as she entertains with powerful and heartfelt stories and helps educate people with her nonfiction books.

Originally from New York, Lynn currently lives in Southern California with her loving and supportive husband.

Please visit *www.lynnmiclea.com* for more information.

BOOKS BY LYNN MICLEA

Fiction

New Contact

Transmutation

Journey Into Love

Ghostly Love

Guard Duty

Loving Guidance

The Diamond Murders

The Finger Murders

The Sticky-Note Murders

Short Story Collections

Beyond the Abyss – Science Fiction

Beyond Terror – Thrillers, Horror, and Suspense

Beyond Love – Love and Romance

Beyond Connections – Family and Relationships

Non-Fiction

Grammar Tips & Tools

Ruthie: A Family's Struggle with ALS

Mending a Heart: A Journey Through Open-Heart Surgery

Unleash Your Inner Joy – Volume 1: Peace

Unleash Your Inner Joy – Volume 2: Abundance

Unleash Your Inner Joy – Volume 3: Healing

Unleash Your Inner Joy – Volume 4: Spirituality

Children's Books

Penny Gains Confidence

Sammy and the Fire

Sammy Visits a Hospital

Sammy Meets Grandma

Sammy Goes to the Dog Park

Sammy Falls in Love

Sammy and the Earthquake

Sammy Goes On Vacation

Wish Fish: Book 1 – Discovering the Secret

Wish Fish: Book 2 – Endless Possibilities

ONE LAST THING...

Thank you for reading this collection of short stories, and I hope you loved them!

If you enjoyed this book, I'd be very grateful if you would post a short review on Amazon. Your support really makes a big difference and helps me immensely!

Simply click the "leave-a-review" link for this book on Amazon, and leave a short review. It would mean a lot to me!

Thank you so much for your support—it is very appreciated!

Thank You!

Printed in Great Britain
by Amazon

28167673R00109